Step-Chain

All over the country children go to stay with step-parents, stepbrothers and stepsisters at the weekends. It's just like an endless chain. A step-chain. *Changing My Name* is the twelfth link in this step-chain.

I'm Eleanor. My mum's just got remarried and I love living in my new family. What I *don't* like is having to go to my dad's. I feel out of place there, and I don't think it's right that he still tries to rule over me. It's like with my name – I want to change it, but Dad won't let me. *Why can't he see how important it is?*

Collect the links in the step-chain! You never know who you'll meet on the way . . .

Step-Chain

CHANGING MY NAME

Ann Bryant

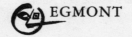
EGMONT

First published in Great Britain 2003
by Egmont Books Limited
239 Kensington High Street
London W8 6SA

Copyright © 2003 Ann Bryant
Series conceived and created by Ann Bryant
Cover illustration copyright © 2003 Mark Oliver

The moral rights of the author and cover illustrator have
been asserted

Series editor: Anne Finnis

ISBN 1 4052 0655 1

1 3 5 7 9 10 8 6 4 2

Typeset by Avon DataSet Ltd, Bidford on Avon, B50 4JH
(www.avondataset.co.uk)
Printed and bound in Great Britain by
Cox & Wyman Ltd, Reading, Berkshire

CONTENTS

Step-Chain

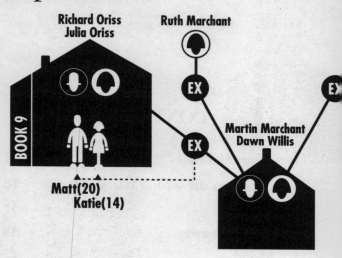

Richard Oriss
Julia Oriss

Ruth Marchant

Martin Marchant
Dawn Willis

EX

EX

EX

Matt(20)
Katie(14)

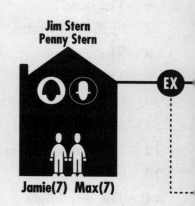

Jim Stern
Penny Stern

EX

Jamie(7) Max(7)

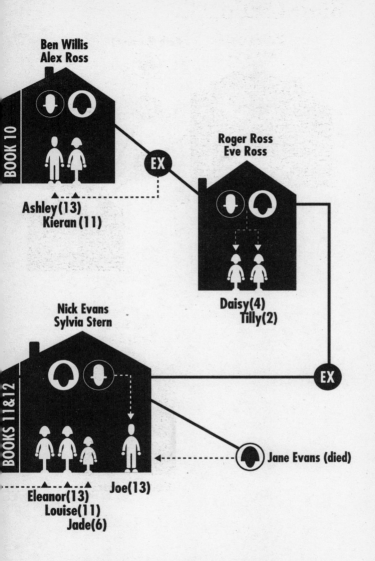

Read on to discover all the links . . .

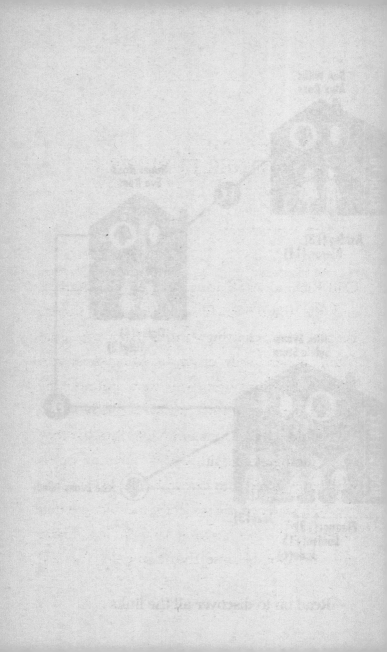

1 ANGER BUBBLES

Cliff Richard was blaring out from the speakers and the room was filled with happy noises. People were chatting, eating and drinking. Mum in her lovely cream wedding dress and Nick in his silvery grey suit were amongst the couples dancing in romantic slow clinches.

I could tell by Mum and Nick's lips that they were singing along with Cliff's romantic words while they gazed into each other's eyes. Yuk!

As I watched them I felt the old familiar bubbles of anger starting to pop just under my ribs. Not because they'd just got married

– I was totally cool with that. I love them both like mad.

No, it's just my stupid hang-up.

It all started about two weeks ago in our kitchen at home. Well, actually it didn't. It started long before that, but it came to a head two weeks ago.

Mum and I were sitting at the table. She was testing me on my French future tense, only she seemed to be doodling at the same time. I couldn't see properly because her arm was in the way. Then she got up to put the kettle on and I saw that she'd written *Sylvia Stern*, which is her name, and then beside it *Sylvia Evans*, which is what she'd be called if she decided to change to Nick's name when they were married.

It's funny, but I'd never thought about that before, and it was only then that I clicked.

'Oh, yeah . . .' I said, my brain slowly

moving away from French verbs and getting into marriages. 'You won't be Sylvia Stern any more, will you?'

Mum laughed. 'Don't look so shocked, love!'

'I'm not.'

And I wasn't. I mean, we all know lots of people change their name when they get married. It was just that for some unknown reason I'd never thought it through in connection with Mum until now. It was going to be so weird. In two weeks time I'd have a different surname from my own mum.

She came back to the table with cups of tea for both of us and asked me what the French for *I will give* was, but I couldn't concentrate any more because the words *Nick and Sylvia Evans* were dancing about inside my brain, blotting out everything else.

In the end, when I kept on coming out with wrong answers, Mum said I ought to give it a break and try again later, so I went up to my room and sat on the floor leaning against my bed. Through the bedroom wall I could hear my stepbrother, Joe, practising his guitar. It sounded really good.

I started reciting all the names in this family in my head – Nick Evans, Sylvia Evans, Joe Evans, Eleanor Stern, Louise Stern, Jade Stern. But I don't want to be a Stern, and I don't want Louise and Jade to be Sterns either. I want all of us to have the same surname – Evans. This is where we live, after all. This family is our main family. Louise and Jade and I only go over to Dad's once a fortnight at the weekend, and *I* only go over on the Sunday these days, because it's got so boring lately and Dad treats me like a baby.

As I sat there listening to Joe's guitar, something suddenly hit me. I didn't know why I hadn't thought of it straight away. I leapt to my feet and belted downstairs to the kitchen.

Mum was loading the dishwasher.

'Can I change my name too, to Evans, like you, Mum?' I blurted out. Then I stood there all tense and excited, shoulders hunched like a little kid, waiting for her to turn round, break into a big smile and say, *Of course you can, darling. I'm so pleased you want to be like me.*

But she didn't even turn round, just started wiping the draining board. 'I don't think your dad'd be very impressed with that idea, love!'

I watched as thin swirls of soapy water swished out from the J-cloth, and felt the anger bubbles burst inside me for the first time.

'You don't seem to realise — this is a big important thing to me, Mum. Can you just ask Dad?'

She did turn round then, but it was obvious she'd already decided my idea was no good. 'Well, I can always ask him, I suppose, but –'

'Can you phone him straight away?'

'You *are* keen, aren't you?' she said, shaking her head, with a little smile on her face. 'I shouldn't raise your hopes, Ellie. I can tell you now the answer will be no.'

'But why do we always have to do what Dad says? He's not in charge, *you* are.'

'You can't just go ahead and do something like that without even consulting Dad. He'd be really upset.'

'What about *me*? *I'll* be really upset if I don't change it.'

'Well, I'll mention it to him next time I phone him, but not tonight. It's too late.'

I had to be satisfied with that for the moment. But there was something else I wanted to sort out too.

'Have you phoned Tasha's mum about me staying there while you and Nick are on your honeymoon?'

Mum started putting things away in the corner cupboard. 'I . . . er . . . decided it would be a bit much asking Tasha's mum to have you for three days.'

'Oh *Mum*!' I started to wail.

'She works full time, Ellie . . . and it isn't fair on her, especially when you've got a perfectly good father who always loves to see you –'

'Oh *no*! Don't tell me you've arranged for me to stay at Dad's. I don't believe it!'

'Well, Jade and Louise are going to be there. And as Dad said, it's sensible to have the three of you under the same roof.'

I was furious. Dad *again*! 'I bet it was him who said I wasn't allowed to stay at Tasha's, wasn't it, and you're just making it up about Tasha's mum working full time and everything?'

'We sorted it out together, Dad and I.'

But I didn't believe her. There's a girl at school called Mel whose parents are divorced, and she once told me that if her dad didn't get his own way as far as she and her brother and sister were concerned, he just gave her mum less money. I've got the feeling Dad might be doing that too. Mel said it happens in all split families. I once asked Mum about it but she went tight-lipped and said it was none of my business, which makes me even more sure I'm right.

'He really does my head in, Mum, laying the law down all the time. It's so unfair. I'm not a baby. I'm thirteen years old and I don't even get a say in where I'm staying while you're away.'

'Calm down, Ellie. It's decided and that's that. Anyway, I bet you'll have a great time. Dad's planned some really fun things.'

'Oh halleluiah! They might be fun things if you're six like Jade, or seven like the twins, but I'm telling you, they are *not* fun for me.'

Mum got a bit stressy then. 'Well, Louise always loves being at Dad's – and she's only eighteen months younger than you.'

I went mad. 'That's because she's that kind of person – all shy and quiet. Oh come on, Mum! I told you how embarrassing it is the way

Dad treats me, giving me a set bedtime on a Saturday night and not letting me stay in the house on my own. I can't even have Tash over because . . .' I went off into a *blah blah blah* voice . . . 'I can see her any time.'

Mum sighed and looked suddenly tired. She pursed her lips and I knew there was no point in saying anything else for now. I also knew I'd hit the nail on the head. It *was* Dad who was behind all this.

I scowled and shut the door a bit harder than usual.

And here we were two weeks later at Mum and Nick's wedding. Dad has got his own way in everything. Even though I've pestered and pestered Mum, I'm definitely not allowed to change my name because he says I can't, *and* I've got to suffer three whole days being treated like a baby and doing 'fun' (ha ha!) things because Dad thinks it's better that we're all three under the same roof. And now Sylvia Evans, with her brand new name, is dancing with her brand new husband while her daughter, Eleanor Stern, sits and watches.

'Don't look so miserable – it may never happen.'

Joe, my stepbrother, came to sit beside me.

'I'm not miserable. I was just thinking about . . . something.'

He leaned forward so he could get a better look at my face. 'God, Ellie, you're still doing your head in about changing your name, aren't you?'

Got it in one, Joe.

It was no wonder. I'd gone on and on about it to him enough times. But I'd also had a pact with myself to try and be sensible and grown up and not say a single word about it, or even think about it on this special day. Only now Joe had brought it up I couldn't help blurting out my fierce thoughts.

'It's my stupid father's pathetic attitude.'

Joe didn't answer. Instead he nudged me and grinned. 'Look!'

I glanced up. A streak of pale blue crumpled silk circled the outside of the room then plunged into the middle, and above the dulcet tones of Cliff came the high pitched voice of my little sister, Jade.

'Can I have a dance on your feet, Nick?'

'Dance on my feet? What *are* you on about?'

I could see Mum smiling as she stepped back from Nick, but I couldn't hear what she said to him.

'She's totally nutty, that girl,' grinned Joe.

'Come on, Nick. I'll show you!' Jade said bossily.

Mum went over to talk to her friend Diane Anderson and Joe and I watched Jade stand on Nick's feet and clutch him round the waist. Nick pretended she was so heavy he couldn't move his feet at all. Then, just when she was least expecting it, he suddenly took off, dancing really quickly all over the place, while Jade giggled her head off.

I couldn't help laughing. 'How does your dad put up with her?'

Joe grinned. 'Dad's drunk. Look at him banging into people!'

'No, he's not. He can't help tottering about! I'd like to see *you* trying to dance with a six-year-old kid standing on your feet!'

'Is that a challenge?'

'Yeah!'

Joe got up and went over. I couldn't hear what he was saying because of the loud music and the noise of everyone talking and laughing. But a moment later Nick came and sat with me. We watched Jade jump on to Joe's feet and we also heard the screech of pain that came out of his mouth.

Nick chuckled. 'Whoa! That'll teach him to be so cocky!'

I giggled.

'Jade's having a great time, isn't she?' he went on.

'Yeah. She's really happy.'

I saw a thoughtful look flit over his face. 'What about Joe? Do you think *he's* happy?'

Nick knows that Joe and I are really close and that Joe would have confided in me if he'd been unhappy about his dad marrying Mum. You see, Joe's mum died about three years ago, and though I'm certain he's totally over it now, he might have been feeling a bit kind of strange on a day like today.

'Joe's absolutely fine, honestly,' I told Nick.

He nodded then looked at me carefully. 'And what about you, Ellie?'

I shrugged.

He grinned. 'I'll interpret that as *Yes, I'm happy except for one thing*.'

Nick is such a cool stepfather. He's nothing like Dad. He never gets on my case about homework or bedtime, or what I wear, or anything. He doesn't tell any of us off or stop us doing stuff. He leaves everything to Mum and just kind of jokes around with me and the others, but whenever anyone needs him, he's always there to help.

Well, nearly always. I'd pestered Nick big time to talk to Mum and get her to make Dad change his mind and let me change my name, and I'd also tried to get him to plead my case about staying at Tasha's. But he wouldn't. You see, Nick doesn't like arguments, not even little tiny ones. I once heard Mum telling Diane that he 'never ever rocks the boat'. And I suppose, if I'm honest with myself, what I wanted him to do would most probably tip the boat right over.

On the other hand, this was his wedding day. He was in a brilliant mood. There wasn't a lot I could do about staying with Dad, because it was a bit late to change that. But changing my name . . . Maybe I'd have one last try.

'Nick?'

'No.'

'What? You don't know what I'm going to ask you.'

'Yes, I do. I can read you like a book, and the answer's no, so shut up about it!'

He kissed me on the nose to show he wasn't mad at me, then went off to find Mum. I wasn't particularly disappointed. I hadn't really expected anything different.

My eyes drifted round the room again and came to rest on my other sister, Louise, who was with two of our cousins, Mandy and Sophie. The cousins were chatting away, giggling and making faces, while Louise just sat there smiling. That's because of her shyness. The only times she isn't shy are when she's at home or when we're at Dad and Penny's.

Dad and Penny have been married for about three years, and I know it sounds weird, but I don't feel as though I know Penny very well, even though I've been seeing her pretty much once a fortnight for all this time. In fact I don't feel as though I know Dad any more either. It's such a false situation when we're over there – like they're trying too hard to make it a cosy family, only it's not working. Not for me, anyway.

Penny's got seven-year-old twins, Max and Jamie, from when she was married before she met Dad. Jade thinks it's wonderful having the twins to play with, and Louise absolutely loves being surrounded by little ones. She doesn't care at all about not seeing her own friends from Saturday morning till Sunday evening once a fortnight.

But me, I don't want this spare family. In fact I wish I could put a solid frame round my *real* family – Mum, Nick, Joe, Louise, Jade and me. And no blurring at the edges where Louise and Jade and I have to keep going over to Dad's.

I glanced at the clock. In less than an hour

Dad would be picking us up. My whole body groaned at the thought of living in the wrong frame for three days.

2 LIVING IN THE WRONG FRAME

It was such an anticlimax waving Mum and Nick off, then the wedding party kind of dissolving as all the guests started to go, and finally the three of us getting into Dad's car, clutching our bags. Louise and Jade sat in the back chatting away like mad while I sat silently in the front, staring out of the side window, even though there was nothing to see because it was practically dark.

'It sounds like you've had a fantastic day!' Dad said in his over-the-top cheerful voice.

'Yes, it was really cool, wasn't it, Ellie?' said Louise.

She didn't like me staying quiet. She wanted me to join in with the conversation, I could tell.

'Uh-huh,' I replied without looking round.

'Well, hopefully you're going to have another one tomorrow,' Dad went on with a little hint of mystery in his voice.

Oh, here we go!

'What? What?' screeched Jade, kicking the back of my seat in her excitement.

'Can you put your feet down, Jade?' I said a bit snappily.

'Ha-*ha*!' said Dad. 'You'll have to wait and see.'

'Give us a clue,' said Louise.

'Hm . . .' said Dad. 'Well, think *favourite food* for a start.'

'Hey, cool! Are we going to have a Chinese take-away?' asked Louise at the top of her voice.

'Got it in one!' laughed Dad.

Louise and Jade broke into big whoops of delight while I shrank into my seat and wished they'd shut up. It was embarrassing. What was so great about having a Chinese take-away? Anyway, it was obvious that Dad was trying to make up for not letting me change my name by doing stuff to please me. Everyone knows that Chinese food is my favourite.

'What else?' asked Jade.

'You'll have to see tomorrow, won't you?' Dad replied, still in his stupid secretive voice.

Can't wait.

The twins were in bed when we got to Dad's. Penny greeted us at the door with a big smile.

'Hello, everybody. Well? Was it wonderful?'

'Yes,' said Jade, skipping past her. 'It was more wonderful than the most wonderful wedding in the whole wide world!'

'Wow!' laughed Penny. 'Well, you can't beat that! What about you two? Have you had a great day?'

Louise nodded, her cheeks going all pink

and her eyes twinkling like mad. 'Mum looked beautiful.'

I didn't say anything. I just did the smallest smile possible and we all trooped through to the living-room.

'This is Jade going down the aisle,' said Louise, breaking into an imitation of Jade in a complete daydream, slowing down and staring round, then suddenly realising she'd been left behind and rushing to catch up.

Dad and Penny were in stitches.

'And this is me dancing,' said Jade, not caring that everyone was laughing – well, nearly everyone. I was determined not to let Dad and Penny think for one second that I was enjoying being with them. I must admit, though, there was a little nagging voice telling me not to be so horrible to Penny, because it was Dad who was stopping me changing my name, and Dad who'd made me come over here while Mum and Nick were away, and Dad who treats me like a baby. On the other hand, Penny must be just as much to blame. She's married to him, after all.

Jade stood on Dad's feet just like she'd done with Nick and Joe. 'Come on, dance!' she instructed him bossily.

I looked at Dad's face. He was only just managing to stay cheerful. Jade, in her excitement, was forgetting that Dad's not the same as Joe and Nick. With Dad you have to be more careful and more polite and think before you speak, in case you're just about to say something that might make him cross. And most of all you have to remember that *he's* in charge. *He* makes the decisions.

'You're going to mess up your dad's shoes!' laughed Penny. But I reckon she meant *You'd better get off because your dad doesn't like having people standing on his feet, and you certainly won't catch him dancing around – he'd feel too much of a twit.*

Jade must have suddenly recognised the tone

of voice. She jumped off instantly and her eyes went big.

'Right, bedtime,' said Dad in a firm voice.

I wasn't at all tired, but going to bed would be better than having to make conversation.

''Night, everybody,' I said, heading for the door.

'Oh . . .' Dad sounded a bit taken aback. 'Right . . .' Then he broke into a big beam. 'See you in the morning, then. Bright and early!'

I didn't answer.

'You go next, Louise!' I heard Jade say in a hyper voice as I went out. 'And the youngest one goes last!'

A few minutes later I was lying in the little put-up bed in 'my' room. It's actually a cubbyhole room that's really an office. There are a couple of posters of mine on the walls, which I brought over from home ages ago when I used to like coming here. As the oldest I got first choice of where I wanted to sleep, and I chose this room because I prefer to be on my own. Louise and Jade sleep in the spare room.

My school bag was by the desk. I could just make out its shape. It felt odd seeing it here, because we've hardly ever been at Dad and Penny's on a school day. Monday and Tuesday were going to be so weird, but I was glad it was term time not holiday time. Going to school would at least get me out of the house.

Another thing that was going to be strange would be seeing Joe at school when we hadn't had breakfast together. It'd be like turning back the clocks to over six months ago, before he and his dad moved in with us. What a terrible time that was. Joe had absolutely hated moving in and I'd tried to be nice because I'd felt sorry for him. But then he'd acted so horribly to Louise that I'd declared war. All that seems like ancient history now.

I pulled the duvet up and buried myself further down.

'Night, Mum. 'Night Nick. Happy honeymoon.

When I woke up on Sunday morning a sinking feeling came over me. If only I could just go back to sleep and wake up on Tuesday! But as I sat up and rubbed my eyes, I realised that I was really hungry, so I got washed and dressed quickly and went downstairs.

They were all in the kitchen eating breakfast.

'Good morning, Mrs Lazy!' Jade greeted me.

'That's a bit unfair,' laughed Dad.

The twins grinned like mad.

'We heard you come up to bed,' Jamie informed me.

'We were still awake,' added Max.

I managed a smile, but already I was feeling irritated. The whole situation here just felt so false.

'Help yourself to cereal, Ellie,' said Penny, 'and then we've got chocolate croissants.'

I knew I was supposed to be ever so grateful,

because chocolate croissants are my very favourite breakfast. But I didn't feel grateful, I just felt my irritation getting worse because it was obvious that this was another example of Dad trying to get round me. I deliberately didn't look up or say anything as I tipped muesli into a bowl.

'Can I get down, Mum?' asked Jamie. 'I want to show Ellie my headstand.'

'What, straight after breakfast?' said Dad.

'It might be better to let your food –' Penny started to say, but it was too late. Jamie had pushed open the kitchen door and was proudly balancing on his head in the hall, where it was carpeted.

'I can stay up longer!' said Max, rushing out and sticking his head down just behind Jamie.

I glanced at Louise. She'd got this soppy look on her face as though she was the twins' mum or something. It made me feel very lonely all of a sudden. It would have been so much better if she'd rolled her eyes at me, and we'd gone upstairs at the first opportunity and whispered about how bored we were, and how we hated being here.

Max crashed down first. He jumped up, pretending he wasn't bothered, and went back to his place at the table.

'Ellie and Lou-lou and Jade are visiting us for three whole days this time, aren't they, Jim?' he asked Dad in an over-the-top voice.

It was Penny who answered. 'That's right,' she said, still wearing her big grin, 'but I wouldn't exactly call them visitors.'

'What are they then?' asked Jamie, coming down from his handstand.

Here we go again! If only I could block my ears.

'They're part of the family, of course,' said Penny brightly.

Louise's face went all pink and smiley, and Jade chose that moment to get out of her place and lean against Dad, so his arm went round her and held her close.

I pretended to read the back of the cereal packet so no one could see how unimpressed I was.

'Come outside and look what I can do, Ellie,' Max suddenly said, grabbing my hand and trying to haul me to my feet.

'No thanks.'

Louise looked embarrassed. She wanted me to be friendlier. 'Well, *I* don't mind coming out,' she said, practically skipping over to the door.

'No, I think Ellie's right,' said Penny. 'It's a bit chilly out there now.'

Oh, stop trying to please me all the time.

'It's not because it's cold — I just don't feel like it.'

There was a silence. I could feel everyone's eyes on me.

Penny spoke in motherly, soothing tones to

Max. 'You can show Ellie later, darling.'

Louise's cheeks were sucked right in. She always does that when she's really anxious about something. Her eyebrows were all arched and her eyes were flashing cross little messages at me.

'I think I'll go and read for a bit,' I said calmly.

Jade got up and looked as though she was about to say something.

'On my own,' I said pointedly.

'But we're going to the motor museum, aren't we, Mum?' said Jamie. 'Ellie hasn't got time to read, has she?'

The anger bubbles were gathering.

'There's no hurry. If Ellie wants to read for a bit, that's fine.'

Dad rubbed his hands together and beamed round at everyone. 'What about helping me get the picnic ready while we're waiting?'

'Yeah!' cried the twins.

I didn't look at anyone as I went out, but it

all went silent again and I guessed that Dad and Penny would be exchanging glances.

3 THE PLAN

I didn't feel like reading, but there was nothing else to do. As I pulled my book out of my school bag, my French vocab book fell out on to the floor. I picked it up and stared at it.

Eleanor Stern
French vocabulary

Pop! went the anger bubbles. *Eleanor Stern*. I don't want that name. I hate the sight of it on the front of my school books. Why should Dad have the final say about something that has nothing to do with him? It's *my* name. I've got to live with it. I pulled all my other school books out in a temper and spread them around me on the carpet. My brand new notebook was lying amongst them. I grabbed a pen, turned the cover back and carefully wrote *Eleanor Evans* on the top of the first page.

The initials were so cool – *E. E.* I wrote them on my hand, then rolled up my jeans and wrote them on my ankle. I'd done this quite a few times in the last few weeks, but it was only at this moment that something hit me.

What if I just went ahead and changed my name on my school books without asking anyone's permission? When my friends saw it I'd just say that was my new name, and when the teachers saw it I'd say exactly the same thing. There'd be nothing that either Mum or Dad could do about it. They'd *have* to let me change it properly after that. It was a brilliant idea!

As I scooped up all my books and put them

away I worked out a plan. Sticky labels were what I needed – enough for all my books and files. I'd go and ask Dad if we could go to Canterton instead of the motor museum. There were always a few shops open on a Sunday. He was sure to say yes if the Chinese take-away and the chocolate croissants were anything to go by. Anyway, I'd say the labels were for school.

'Hey, that was quick!' said Louise, looking happy as I went back into the kitchen.

She was helping Dad make sandwiches for the picnic, while Penny was clearing away the breakfast things. The twins came bursting into the kitchen as I opened my mouth to speak.

'Can we go into Canterton today, Dad? There's something I need for school.'

He was at the sink. I didn't miss the look he exchanged with Penny. The smile dropped off Jamie's face. 'We can't, can we, Jim, because of the motor museum.'

I felt like throttling the kid. Why didn't he mind his own business? And anyway, the thought of spending the day at a boring motor museum wasn't exactly filling me with joy. The twins might think it was wonderful, but it wouldn't be any fun for me, and probably not for the other two either.

Dad must have seen my scowly face. 'There's a lovely picnic area and an adventure playground in the grounds, you know, Ellie. It's not just a motor museum.'

'Adventure playground! Cool!' Jade said.

'I think they've even got peacocks there,' Penny added.

Louise broke into a big smile. 'Hey, wow!'

Anyone'd think Penny had said there was a stage with ten top bands playing.

I tried to keep calm and speak in a sensible voice. 'That's OK, I'll go into town on my own.'

'What exactly do you need for school?' Penny asked me.

Maybe I'd better not say name labels in case I got quizzed.

'Files.' It wasn't till I said it that I realised how clever I'd been. 'And name labels.'

'No problem,' said Penny. 'I can get them for you tomorrow.'

'I really need them *for* tomorrow.'

Louise was glancing anxiously from Dad to Penny and back.

Dad frowned then spoke in his firm voice. 'We'll stop at Smiths on the way. That's the answer.'

Suddenly I'd had enough.

'But why do I have to come to the motor museum? I'll be so bored.'

Louise sucked her cheeks in.

Dad's eyes flashed. The horrible strict layer that lives underneath was pushing through this false, nice layer on top. 'Because I'm not happy about leaving you to your own devices for a whole day while we're out.'

'We're all allowed to choose what CD we want in the car, Ellie,' Jade interrupted. 'And we're going to play games too, and there's a massive gift shop that's as enormous as the downstairs of this house –' she spread her arms wide, then dropped her voice to an excited whisper – '*and* Dad's giving us extra pocket money to spend in there!'

So Dad and Penny had made a great job of convincing Jade that we were in for the best day of our lives. I knew there was no point in arguing. Dad would never change his mind.

Penny must have suddenly felt sorry for me. 'Let's compromise,' she said, 'and come back early from the motor museum.'

'Yeah, and play Trillial Perstute,' cried Jade at the top of her voice.

The others cracked up.

'It's Trivial Pursuit!' said Jamie, giving Jade a *dur* look.

'That's what I said,' Jade protested.

'So what time will we be back?' I asked

'About three.'

Could be worse.

4 THE TAKE-AWAY

It was actually a quarter to six when we got back, and I was dying to have some time on my own. The twins' loud voices had been getting on my nerves all day. I'm not the least bit interested in old cars, so listening to them asking Dad question after question as we wandered round the museum was about as much fun as peeling potatoes. To make it worse, Louise and Jade were all chummy with Penny so I felt like the one left over, especially when we passed a group of girls and boys of my age all hanging out together, laughing and mucking about. I'm sure they were pitying me for having to trail round with my family. I'd felt like yelling out *Look, they're not my family, OK?*

I didn't quite make it to my room because the moment we got in the house Jade dragged me into the living-room to help her do a headstand. She'd been on and on about it in the car on the way home and I knew I wasn't going to get any peace until she'd cracked it.

'Right, hold my legs, Ellie,' she said, kicking her feet violently up in the air. But she just toppled into a forward roll before I had the chance.

'Would you like some music on, Ellie?' asked Penny brightly.

The last time I'd looked Penny and Dad didn't have any CDs that I liked, but at least it would get me out of the headstand coaching. So I went to choose something while the others all tried to find ways of stopping Jade from tumbling into a forward roll.

Curled up in the chair, listening to the CD, I found myself looking at Penny. She was wearing jeans, a black top and lots of chunky silver jewellery. I thought how young and fashionable she looked, and I got a flashback to our open day at school. When my friends saw her they'd all said how lucky I was having such a trendy stepmum, but I didn't want her even to be there. I knew I wasn't the only one from a 'fragmented' family, as our tutor calls it, but I was the only one with two sets of parents at open day, and I hated it.

My thoughts were suddenly interrupted by Max's loud voice. 'Can *you* read me my story tonight, Ellie?'

'Aah!' cooed Louise. 'Isn't that sweet, El?'

I made a vague noise that could have been 'Mm.'

'And Lou-lou can do mine!' said Jamie, clapping his hands together, as though he'd just found out that Father Christmas had a big brother.

'Course we can, can't we, Ell?'

'Then that'll be one sister each,' announced Max.

My whole body tensed up. I wasn't their sister. Why did they have to go on about it all the time?

'And who's going to read to *me*?' asked Jade, pouting.

'I'll read to you,' said Dad. 'But first, what about this Chinese?' He rubbed his hands together and looked round brightly.

'I'm not hungry.'

Dad looked a bit taken aback but didn't sound at all stressy. 'It'll be nearly half an hour before we get to eat it. I expect you'll be hungry by then.'

'Anyway, it's ages since we had lunch,' said Louise, throwing me a look which said, *Stop being so grumpy*. 'You *must* be hungry!'

'Ellie's in a bad mood,' Jade announced calmly as she fiddled with the velcro on her shoe, tearing it apart and sticking it together over and over again.

The noise seemed to echo in the little silence that followed her words, and my temper snapped.

'Look, I'm just not hungry, OK?'

A look passed between Penny and Dad.

'No problem,' said Dad in his tight voice, which means he's cross but he's trying not to show it. 'I'll go and order one of the set menus.'

I mumbled that I was going to read and as I got up to leave the room I could feel Louise's eyes on me, and knew without looking that her cheeks would be sucked right in.

Upstairs I lay on my mattress and stared at the ceiling, my hands behind my head, the anger bursting inside me. I was cross with myself for being cross with everyone else, and cross with everyone else for making me so cross. If only I could go home to my proper family. Right now.

Then I suddenly remembered my brand new

files and name labels. A lovely feeling of excitement swished through my body at the thought of covering my old name with my new one, and I went racing off downstairs to get the Smiths bag from the hall.

Jade must have heard me because she was out of the living-room in a flash. 'Come and watch me, Ellie. I can *do* one now!'

'I'm busy.'

But she followed me upstairs and spent the next ten minutes doing headstands in my room. And when I finally got rid of her, the twins came up and the three of them played at taxis on the landing right outside my door until Penny called them all down.

'Jim'll be back in a few minutes with the Chinese,' she said.

My stomach did an enormous rumble at the sound of the words, and I realised I was starving hungry. What an idiot I'd been to say I didn't want any.

'What are you doing?'

I hadn't heard Louise come in. It gave me a shock to see her standing at the door, all friendly and back to normal. That was typical of her. She never bears a grudge.

'Nothing much.'

'Dad's gone to pick up the Chinese. He'll be back in a minute. I'm laying the table in the kitchen. Do you want chopsticks or knife and fork or just a fork?'

Why was she asking me this when I'd clearly said no? Was it some kind of trick? 'Erm . . . I said I wasn't going to have any, remember?'

'Dad thought you might change your mind when you saw it. He's getting enough for you too.'

I wasn't sure what to do. Should I stick to my guns and starve, or give in, which would be like accepting some of Dad's niceness? I tried to look as though I couldn't much care either way. 'I'll have a bit then. Knife and fork 'll do.'

'OK. And afterwards we're playing Trivial Pursuit, remember. Dad and the twins against Penny and us two. Jade's going to shake the dice and move the counter things. And Ellie . . .' She was still hovering around '. . . can you be a bit . . . you know, like, nicer to the twins?'

I didn't get the chance to say anything because she zipped off so quickly.

A couple of minutes later I heard Dad come in.

'It's ready, Ellie.' Penny called upstairs.

I felt pretty embarrassed going into the kitchen and had to concentrate hard on not showing it.

'Can you get the spare chair from the hall, Max?' Penny asked him.

'I thought Ellie wasn't having any,' Jade immediately piped up.

'She's changed her mind,' Penny replied firmly. 'Fetch the paper serviettes from the top drawer, can you, Jade?'

I could feel Jade's eyes on me as she went to do as she was told. She must have picked up from Penny's tone of voice that it would be naughty to say anything else, but she also sensed the awkward atmosphere and it was intriguing her.

Apart from everyone saying how lovely the meal was, no one talked as we ate, and by the time we'd finished, the embarrassing atmosphere had gone, thank goodness.

I just had to get through the game of Trivial Pursuit then the day would be over. And the next day was Monday. A brand new week.

A brand new name.

5 MONDAY

It was such a relief to go to school on Monday and be with my friends. Ever since Mum and Nick had driven off, I'd been dying to see my best friend Tasha. I could have phoned her on my mobile, but I wanted to talk properly, face to face, so I'd just texted her to say that I'd tell her all about the wedding and everything at school.

The moment the bell went for morning break, we stuffed our books away and headed outside.

'Tell me everything!' she said, linking her arm through mine as we swung out of the year eight door.

I started with the wedding. In big detail.

'You're so lucky,' Tasha kept saying. 'I wish *my* mum'd get married.'

'She's already married!' I spluttered.

'Yeah, but . . .'

Poor Tasha. She looked so depressed. I put my arm round her for a moment. 'Is it really bad at home?'

She shrugged. It's just the same as usual. Loads of arguments. Loads of awful atmospheres. Yesterday I went down to the rec on my own just to get away. I finished up on a swing for about half an hour. When I got back, Dad had gone out, thank God, and Mum was all bristly and snappy with nasty piggy eyes, so I went up to my room and listened to my Eva Cassidy CD and that made me even more depressed.'

I squeezed Tasha's shoulder. 'Poor you.'

She tried to smile. 'What did *you* do yesterday anyway? How's it going at your dad's?'

I felt a bit guilty complaining about being at Dad's because in one way it wasn't half as bad as what Tasha was having to put up with. But in another way it was worse. *I* couldn't even go off to the rec on my own.

'He's trying to be all nice to make up for not letting me change my name, and not letting me stay at your place while Mum and Nick are away. We had chocolate croissants for breakfast yesterday and Chinese take-away in the evening.'

She grinned. 'So at least the food's OK.'

'Yeah, but that's about all. I mean, guess where we went yesterday?' I didn't give her the chance. 'Their idea of a fun day out – a motor museum with an adventure playground that had five-year-olds playing in it!'

Tasha rolled her eyes.

I went on to tell her how bad the rest of the day had been, but there was one bit I didn't mention – the labels. I'm not totally sure why I kept quiet about that, because Tasha knows how much I hate being called Eleanor Stern. But there was a little voice inside me saying, *Don't tell her till you've done it, in case she tries to talk you out of the idea.*

I'd planned to do the labels last night, but Jade had gone to bed after our game of Trivial Pursuit and she'd had a nightmare about me falling down a hole. She'd woken up crying and begged me to sleep in the same room as her, so Louise and I had swapped rooms for the night, and I'd decided to leave the labels until I was completely alone. I was definitely going to do them later today, then I'd show Tasha tomorrow. Another thrill of happiness zipped through my body at the thought of my new name being on all my books and files.

At lunch time I saw Joe with his friends in the dinner queue.

'Are you having a nice time at Dean's?' I asked him.

'Nah, rubbish,' said Joe. He was mucking

about because Dean was right behind him. 'What's it like at your dad's?'

'The pits. Yesterday we went to a motor museum. Need I say more?'

Joe threw me a quick look of sympathy. He realised I was acting as though I wasn't bothered because we were surrounded by friends. And we both knew that once we were back home we'd talk about it properly.

'I didn't know there was a motor museum round here,' said Dean.

'There isn't. It's miles away. And we had to listen to stories all the way there to keep Jade's mind off being sick.'

Joe grinned. 'Good old Jade.' Then he shrugged. 'Oh well, back to the madhouse tomorrow!'

I got a lovely feeling when he said that because I'd soon be stepping back into the right picture with its strong frame keeping it safely in place.

'Where've they been then?' asked Andy, another of Joe's friends.

Joe clicked straight away that Andy was talking about Mum and Nick. 'Venice.'

'I bet they're having a really cool time,' said Tasha. 'I can just imagine them going down cobbled streets, and sitting with their arms round each other in gondolas, and gazing into each other's eyes in romantic candlelit restaurants.'

The boys were looking at her as though she was totally insane, except that we all know Tasha is a very expressive type of person. That's why I like her so much.

Andy went cross-eyed and groaned.

'Leave my friend alone,' I said, putting my arm round Tasha. I guessed she was probably imagining how great it would be if her own parents acted like that.

When we sat down with the rest of our group of friends, Lucy was talking about the

English lesson we'd just had.

'I don't get the homework,' she said. 'It's a stupid poem, and I don't know what I'm going to write about.'

I was quite glad she'd said that because I didn't really understand the homework either.

'It's easy,' said Rachel. 'You just go on about what you think T. S. Eliot might have been thinking when he wrote that poem. It doesn't have to be what he was *really* thinking. That's the great thing about English, remember? You can make up what you want. It's not like maths. There's no such thing as a wrong answer, because it's only someone's opinion.'

'He's got a funny name, hasn't he,' said Tasha, 'the guy in the T. S. Eliot poem? I mean, fancy being called Alfred J. Poofrock.'

Everyone except me creased up.

'It's Alfred J. Prufrock!' said Rachel.

Tasha went a bit red. I felt sorry for her, because I know how stupid you feel when you've made a mistake like that. You're never sure whether to cover it up by saying you were only joking.

'Yeah, but it would still be terrible to have a name like Prufrock,' I said, to try and get the spotlight off Tasha.

'Well, I'd change it if it was me, by — what's it called? — statutory declaration.'

The others had lost interest. But not me. And not Tasha. We exchanged big-eyed looks.

I went for a really casual tone. 'Statutory declaration? What's that? Have you been secretly studying law, Lucy?'

'All I know,' she said with her mouth full, 'is that our next-door neighbour changed her name back to her maiden name when she got divorced. I can remember her telling Mum that she'd been to the solicitor's and handed over a cheque and done it — just like that!'

I didn't say anything. But inside I was thinking that if I saved up loads of pocket money I could do exactly the same thing – just go to a solicitor and change my name without even asking Mum or Dad. Yes, that's what I'd do. Tomorrow I'd change it unofficially, and in a few weeks' time, or however long it took to save up the right amount, I'd do it really properly. Officially.

Legally. I loved that word.

From the moment I got back to Dad's after school I tried to find a time when I could be on my own so I could do my labels, but it was just as though fate was trying to stop me, because things kept getting in the way.

First it was Penny not feeling well and asking me and Louise to make the tea. She still didn't feel well when we were clearing away, so Louise said we'd help the young ones with their baths and getting ready for bed and everything. Then Dad came home and suggested that we all watched a programme about dinosaurs together.

'I've got homework to do,' I said. It was true, I'd suddenly remembered that this was the last night for doing my maths, and it would take me a while because I didn't get it.

'Why not leave it till the end of the programme?' said Dad, giving me an encouraging smile.

'I can't. It's going to take me ages as it is. And I need to phone Tasha to ask her something about it.'

'I'll give you a hand with it afterwards.'

He was smiling but there was a definite look in his eyes that said, *I'm the boss round here*. And you don't argue with that look.

So I sat there watching the stupid dinosaur programme while taking subtle glances at the others. The twins and Jade were in their jamas, all hot and shiny and excited. Once or twice they turned to Dad to ask him something, and I noticed that the look on his face wasn't the same as when he was talking to me. There was no . . . barrier between them.

At the end of the programme Dad helped me with the maths but it still took ages and ages, and afterwards there was a programme about Hollywood that I really wanted to see, and for once I was actually allowed to stay up and watch it. By the time it had finished I was too tired to do the labels. I'd do them tomorrow.

Yes, definitely.

6 THE NEWS

I grew happier and happier all through school on Tuesday as I counted down the hours till I'd be back in the right frame with Mum and Nick. Dad could go and stuff himself. Never again was I going to put up with him controlling me. No one could force me to go over to his place, could they? He'd soon regret being so bossy once he realised he'd driven me away for good.

There was something tapping away in the furthest corner of my brain, reminding me of yesterday evening by flashing up little pictures of Dad frowning at the calculator and scribbling columns of figures trying to sort out the answers to my maths. But every time the pictures started to come into focus I shook them away. I didn't want them there. They didn't fit in with the other pictures of Dad.

It was six-thirty when I started waiting for the phone to ring, because I knew that that was the earliest possible time Mum and Nick could be home from the airport. Penny was upstairs getting the twins ready for bed and Jade was hanging around them, gloating because she didn't have to go to bed. Dad wasn't back from work, and Louise and I were watching telly in the living-room.

'I can't wait!' I blurted out, hugging my knees excitedly at the thought of getting away. 'Can you?'

Louise just shrugged.

I could feel my hackles rising. It had been bad enough putting up with her being full of *Dad this* and *Dad that* for the last two days, but surely she was looking forward to getting back home to her real family?

'Aren't you looking forward to seeing Mum and Nick?'

'Yeah, I am. Only . . .'

I knew I was sounding exasperated. 'What's the matter?'

She sighed a huge sigh. 'I feel sorry for Dad. He's going to miss us. He told me last night.'

'He won't miss me.'

'Yes, he will. He said so.'

Huh! Like he'd say that!

It was a quarter to seven when he came in. 'The traffic! I've been sitting in a jam going mad with frustration.'

Louise went and gave him a big hug. 'Never mind.'

I didn't move.

'Had a good day, Ellie?' He came over and put his arm round my shoulder. It felt stupid and awkward.

'Yes, thanks.'

Then he went off to say hello to the twins and Penny, and I noticed he looked disappointed as he left the room – probably because I hadn't gone over to him like Louise had.

A few minutes later he and Penny came back in together. Dad was carrying a tray with four glasses and a bottle of champagne.

Louise and I stared. What was going on?

'Now,' said Dad, putting the tray down on the little table with a bit of a flourish. 'The twins are in bed and Jade's engrossed in some very important colouring, so I think we're safe for a few minutes.'

I didn't get what was going on.

'I don't want you two to think that this is to celebrate your going,' he carried on in a brighter than bright voice. 'Far from it!'

Penny put her hand on Dad's arm and smiled at me and Louise. They both had a secretive air about them.

Dad unscrewed the metal wire at the top of the champagne bottle and began easing the cork out. 'Better not risk popping it,' he said. 'Don't want any broken windows.'

Penny laughed delightedly, then went suddenly serious as Dad poured the fizzing champagne into the glasses.

'We're not saying anything officially for a while yet . . .' she began hesitantly.

'. . . but,' went on Dad, handing a glass each to me and Louise, 'we wanted you two to be the first to know.'

I glanced at Louise. Her eyes were sparkling more than the bubbly. I didn't like what I was hearing, but I wasn't sure why.

Penny put her glass to one side and spoke very slowly and proudly, 'You two are going to have a half-brother or sister! I'm pregnant!'

'Yeah!' cried Louise. 'I knew it would be that!' Then she put her glass down and gave

Penny a massive hug. They were rocking from side to side, clasping each other and laughing at the same time. Penny had tears in her eyes.

Dad was looking at me. I'd got a fixed grin on my face and was clutching the stem of my glass so tightly that it was a miracle it didn't snap off. Masses of thoughts were whizzing through my head, all to do with surnames and half-brothers and sisters, but there was one big thought: *Maybe Dad'll give me a break once he's got a baby of his very own.*

'Great news, isn't it?' said Dad.

'Y-yes. Congratulations,' I said. 'I never guessed.'

Louise turned round and took my glass off me, put it on the table, then proceeded to give *me* a massive hug while Dad and Penny hugged each other. And it was precisely then that the phone rang.

I made a lurch for it.

'Mum?'

'Hello, love.'

To hear her voice was so brilliant. 'Oh wow! You're back! Are you actually at home right now? Was it good?'

She laughed a really happy laugh. 'Yes, we're back. Yes, we're at home. Yes, it was really really good!'

And next minute Nick had picked up the other phone. 'Hello, Ellie! Been behaving yourself?'

'Hi, Nick! How did you know it was me?'

'Fifty-fifty guess.'

'Did you have the best time?'

'We did. The best!'

'I'll get Dad to drop us off, OK?'

'We're just unpacking and getting sorted out.' That was Mum. 'Dad can drop you back whenever it's convenient. I don't want to interrupt whatever you're all doing. Shall I have a word with him?'

'No, it's OK, we're not doing anything. I'll tell him to bring us now. He won't mind.'

I glanced over and noticed that Louise, Dad and Penny were just kind of standing there, like statues, as though they were waiting for me to come back so we could carry on from exactly where we left off. Louise's statue was wearing a big scowl.

'So they had a good time then,' said Dad, as I went back over.

'Yeah, really brilliant!'

'But isn't it great about Penny and Dad?' said Louise, giving me one of her looks. 'I'm going to propose a toast!' She was trying to make up for me. 'Here's to our new baby sister or brother,' she said, raising her glass and speaking in a bright clear voice.

I didn't like the words she'd chosen. They were messing up my two frames.

We all took a sip – or a gulp in my case, because I wanted to finish the glass so we could get back home. But unfortunately I broke into a fit of coughing.

'Oh dear! A bit too enthusiastic!' said Dad, patting me on the back.

Louise ignored me and spoke to Penny in her new-found bright and bubbly voice. 'When's it due, Penny?'

'Ages! I'm only two months pregnant. We've got seven to go.'

Dad gave her a fond smile. 'But at least you're getting the worst bit over first.'

Louise looked puzzled.

'Penny's been feeling quite sick and tired. It's perfectly usual in the first months of pregnancy.'

'And I'm certainly not touching this stuff!' said Penny, shuddering in an over-the-top way. 'Alcohol! Definite no-no! I just wanted to hold the glass!' She giggled.

'I can't wait to tell everyone!' said Louise, jumping up and down.

She was really getting on my nerves

now going on and on when this wasn't our proper family.

'Actually,' said Penny, 'we'd rather you didn't say anything yet for a while. It's such early days, you see. That's why we didn't tell Jade. We haven't even told the twins. It's just that, as we said, we wanted you two to be the first to know.'

That earned her another hug from Louise, while I took a few more gulps of champagne.

'Can't we even tell Mum?' Louise asked.

'And Nick and Joe?' I blurted out.

Dad looked at me as though I'd suggested telling the local newspaper. 'Let's just keep it to ourselves for a month or so, Ellie.' He was looking at me like he does – in a different way from the way he looks at Louise.

I took another gulp and noticed that Louise's glass was still full. I was about to tell her to get on with it when I realised I was swaying.

'Whoops!' said Dad, putting a hand on my back. 'I probably shouldn't be encouraging my daughters to drink alcohol, but it's such a special occasion.

'I'm OK,' I said, taking a step forwards.

My head was starting to feel a bit funny and I really wanted to sit down, but that might have given him the idea I didn't want to go.

'Hurry up, Louise,' I told her, 'otherwise Jade'll have to go straight to bed as soon as we get back.'

Louise grimaced and took a teeny sip of champagne.

'You don't have to drink it all, Lou-lou,' said Dad. 'It was just so we could have an official family celebration.'

I could feel another cloud of anger bubbles gathering in the pit of my stomach. How dare he talk about us four as though we were a family unit. We weren't. It should be the twins here drinking champagne, not us. They could have had a sip topped up with lemonade, couldn't they?

'I'll take you whenever you're ready,' said Dad quietly.

At long last!

7 IN THE RIGHT FRAME

Everything was back to how it should be. We were all sitting round the kitchen table drinking tea, except Nick who was drinking Italian wine.

'I'm not looking forward to going back to work, I can tell you,' he said, flopping back in his chair and sighing.

Mum flashed him a big smile. 'Just keep thinking about our resolution. That should inspire you.'

'What relosootion?' said Jade.

The rest of us laughed. 'Resolution,' Joe corrected her.

'What resultootion?' she tried again.

'*Resolution*!' we all said at once.

'Nick's going to do loads of overtime, then we'll be able to afford a nice holiday for all of us in the summer.'

My happiness was almost complete. 'Oh, that's a great idea, Mum. Where shall we go?'

'Venice?' suggested Jade, who hadn't heard of all that many holiday locations.

I smiled at her, a nice big smile at the thought of my own personal resolution. It felt as though the last bit of my temper was being put out by lovely cool water. I was where I belonged now, with all the right people. And with a bit of luck I was going to be able to keep it that way for good.

'How about Los Angeles?' suggested Joe.

'Yes, or maybe the Bahamas,' Nick scoffed.

Mum laughed. 'I'll get a few brochures at the weekend and we'll look at prices,' she said.

'Emily's going away to the South of France

in the summer,' said Jade. 'Where *is* the south of France, Mummy? Near the capital of Venice?'

We all creased up. Jade had got so many things confused in her little six-year-old mind.

'It's on top of the Eiffel Tower, I think,' said Joe, which made us laugh even more.

A scowl covered Jade's face. 'Now you're just being silly.'

'We'll look at the globe tomorrow, love,' said Mum.

'But right now,' said Nick, 'we've got something much more exciting to discuss, haven't we, Sylv?'

'It'd better not be bedtime,' said Jade, putting her hands on her hips like a grown-up.

'Nope. That comes up next on the agenda,' said Nick. He leaned over and poked Jade in the tummy. 'But first . . .'

Jade giggled.

'What?' said Joe, scraping his chair as he leaned back and stretched out his legs. 'Don't tell us you won the Italian lottery?'

Mum shook her head, looking secretive and smug. I recognised that look. Where had I seen it very recently? Oh my God! This was amazing! If I was right . . .

The pulse in my stomach started up in a throb. I sat up straighter in my chair, my eyes glued to Mum. She was staring right back at me with a big smile, full of love. She knew I knew. So when she spoke, it was as though she was telling *me*. Just me. I felt so special and honoured, and all the things I hadn't felt an hour ago.

Mum was reaching for Nick's hand, but still she didn't move her eyes away from mine.

'We're going to have a baby,' she said in a soft, proud voice. 'I'm pregnant.'

There was a silence. No, there wasn't. Everyone else was saying stuff in excited, high-pitched voices. It was only me who was silent. I couldn't speak I was so happy. I got up and went round to give Mum a big hug.

'I knew you'd be happy,' she said. 'Did you guess by any chance?'

'No. How could I?'

'Only that I've put on quite a bit of weight and I wondered if it made you put two and two together.'

Jade got up and started dancing round the table. 'I'm going to have a baby sister! I'm going to tell Mrs Taylor in news time. It's going to be so cool at school because now we'll be doing babies as topic work for ages and ages. That's what Mrs Taylor did when Danny Lester told her he was having a baby!'

Joe and Nick broke out in laughter again.

Louise gave Mum a kiss. 'Do you know if it's going to be a boy or a girl?' she asked excitedly.

Mum shook her head. 'No, and I don't want to know. I'd much rather have a surprise.'

Jade started dancing again, and yelling out at the top of her voice, 'Mummy's having twins! Mummy's having twins!' She was getting more and more excited, practically breaking into song. 'Just like Dad and Penny's got!'

At that moment Louise's eyes met mine. She looked as though she was bursting to speak. I gave her a small urgent shake of the head. Thank goodness Dad and Penny had told us not to tell anyone. I wouldn't have been able to bear it if this wonderful family time had suddenly been interrupted by Louise telling everyone about that other baby.

Just to be sure that she got my message loud and clear, I said to Mum, 'Are we allowed to tell people? Or do you want to keep it a secret a while longer?'

Mum stood up and showed us the top of her trousers. They were really tight. 'These are a size bigger than usual and I'm already growing out of them so I don't think there's much chance of keeping it a secret!'

'So when's it due?' I asked, feeling even more excited.

'In about five months. October 16th.'

I glanced at Louise. She was knitting her eyebrows together deep in concentration. I bet I knew what she was trying to work out – how much older Mum's baby was going to be than Penny's.

'Right, bedtime, young lady,' said Mum, putting out a hand and trying to grab Jade as she twizzled and skipped round the kitchen.

'You're going to be very dizzy,' said Nick, getting up to help.

'Jade came to a standstill and threw out her arms dramatically. 'I'm dizzy of happiness!' she said.

And while everyone else laughed I just smiled and thought, *That's exactly how I feel too*.

'What will you call it if it's a girl?' Louise suddenly asked, coming out of her mathematical daydream.

'No, what will you call it if it's a *boy*, more like?' asked Joe.

Mum laughed. 'We truly haven't given names a thought yet.'

A feeling of urgency was prodding me in the stomach. Prodding hard. Nearly stabbing. Mum and Nick might not have decided what to call their baby, but one part of its name *was* decided.

Evans.

Later, when Mum had put Jade to bed and the others were downstairs still talking, I headed up to my room to do my new name labels. The news of the two babies had made me more determined than ever that I was going to change my name. But Louise came chasing after me and caught up with me on the landing.

'Let's go into your room, I so want to talk to you,' she said, grabbing my hand.

She closed the door behind us and plonked herself down on the bed, bouncing a bit. 'Isn't it incredible?' she said in a gasp. 'I was dying to tell everyone about Penny and Dad, weren't you?'

No, I was not.

'I'm glad Mum's baby is due first,' I said, ignoring her question.

'They're only two months apart,' said Louise. 'Just think, they can be friends when they grow up – and go to each other's houses and everything.'

She'd said the worst possible thing. It felt like the more I wanted to keep the families in their separate frames, the more Louise wanted to mingle them up.

'What are you on about, Louise? Dad and Penny's baby won't be anything to do with *our* baby. Mum and Penny aren't friends, you know. They don't even have anything to do with each other.'

Louise looked shocked. 'I only meant that the babies would probably get to know each other because we'll be half-sisters to both of them. You know, we'll be exactly in the middle. Equal.'

With every word she spoke she was making things worse. I had to get her to see things my way. 'How can we be equal when we live here nearly all the time and only go over to Dad's every other weekend?' I didn't add that I was about to stop that as well.

'Well, maybe we'll start going more when the baby's born. We want it to know us just as well as it knows Max and Jamie, don't we?'

'*You* can if you want, but I'm not going to.' I wanted an end to the conversation so I could get on with my labels.

'Look, Louise, I've got homework to do now, OK?'

She sighed a bit huffily and went off. Then after a few seconds I heard her voice. It was coming from Mum and Nick's room. I tiptoed on to the landing and listened. She was on the phone to Dad.

'It's due in October. That's two months before yours, isn't it?'

I gasped. Why was she telling Dad about Mum's baby? It was nothing to do with him.

The next thing I heard made me even more angry. 'Are you *sure* you don't want us to tell anyone about yours? Not even Mum and Nick?'

Right, that did it. I marched into Mum and Nick's room and stood there glaring hard at Louise, my hands on my waist.

'Er . . . actually . . . sorry, Dad. I've got to go now.' She hung up.

'What are you telling Dad about Mum's baby for, Louise? It's Mum and Nick's news. They might not want Dad to know.'

'Mum never said it was a secret.'

'She probably didn't realise you were going to get straight on the phone to Dad about it. You're so stupid, Louise! You don't *think*, do you?'

'Yes, I *do* think. Only *I* think nice thoughts. Not like some people round here!'

I was shocked. This didn't sound like my sweet, shy sister.

'Oh, just . . . shut up!' was all I could think of saying. Then I stomped back to my room and turned my radio on loudly to drown out Louise's horrible words.

But they wouldn't go away. They just sat there, making me furious. There was no way I could do my labels now, thanks to my stupid sister.

8 RISING PANIC

On Wednesdays Mum works. When she's finished she picks Jade up from the Andersons'. Louise, Joe and I come home by bus and usually get back about half an hour before Mum.

The moment we got in I went straight up to my room. The phone was ringing but I ignored it. This time nothing was going to stop me doing my labels.

A minute later Louise was at my bedroom door, looking excited. How could she be acting so normal after our big argument? I didn't get her.

'That was Penny. She was wondering if we'd like to go over this weekend. I said I'd ask Mum when she got back from work.'

My hackles rose. 'She must be joking! We've only just seen them. Why would we want to see them again so soon? *I* certainly don't.'

Louise's cheeks went red and her eyes flashed. 'Well, *I'm* going because I actually care about my dad and my stepmother. Unlike *some* people round here.'

'Look –'

'What are you two arguing about?' interrupted Joe, passing my door.

'We're not arguing!' I snapped.

'OK, OK!' He put his hands up in front of him like he was surrendering. 'What are you talking about then?'

I opened my mouth to reply, but though the words that raced through my mind made sense to me, I had the horrible feeling that Joe wouldn't get where I was coming from any more than anyone else seemed to be doing, so I kept quiet.

Louise was still wearing her hard look. 'Penny wanted to know if we'd like to go over again this weekend, only Ellie doesn't want to, because she hates going to see Dad.'

'Oh . . . right,' said Joe, looking suddenly uncomfortable as though he wished he hadn't asked in the first place.

'Is that OK?' I asked sarcastically. 'Anyone else got any objections to me leading my *own* life?'

Joe shot back into his room. Louise gave me a half-sad, half-cross look, then stomped her way downstairs.

I shut my bedroom door and leaned against it. Nobody understood me, not even Joe. It was a horrible lonely feeling.

Very slowly and carefully I laid out all my school books on the floor. There were thirteen. The teacher had got my geography book so that made fourteen.

Next I took out my brand new sheet of labels and counted them. Twenty. Perfect. I could afford to mess up six. I wrote my new name slowly and carefully with my thickest black pen, so that it came out nice and bold, and I only had to repeat three that were a bit wobbly and one where I did a capital L by mistake. So I'd still got three left over.

Unpeeling the first label and sticking it on my history book felt brilliant. There was no trace of the old name showing through the label at all. I had the thick black pen to thank for that – and also the fact that I'd written in such big lettering.

It took nearly ten minutes to do thirteen perfect ones and press them down really firmly over the old names. When I'd finished I sat back and admired them. They looked brilliant.

Gutted, Dad! Try arguing with that!

Tasha would be the first to see them, then it would gradually spread round my other friends and then the class, and then the teachers. When they asked me about it, I'd just say I'd changed it because of Mum and Nick being married. I hugged my knees imagining the teacher calling the register.

'*Eleanor Evans?*'

'*Yes, miss.*'

The next morning after breakfast I got my bag ready for school, feeling excited about this being the first day of the new me. I pulled out one of my books to have a look at the label, and when I saw it I actually gasped. The writing was massive. So thick and black. Why, oh why, had I done it like that? It looked totally babyish, like something Jade might have written.

I was going to feel such an idiot at school. Everyone would stare at it and comment and the teachers would instantly think I was trying to make some big statement, because that's what teachers are like. Oh my God, what if the head teacher decided to phone up Mum? I could just imagine it.

'Hello, Mrs Stern?'

'It's Mrs Evans, actually. I've just remarried.'

'Oh, congratulations, Mrs Evans. And I see Eleanor has also changed her surname —'

'What?'

'Yes, she's daubed it in thick black pen all over the front of her school books.'

'She's what?'

'I thought I ought to check—'

'My daughter has definitely not changed her name. I'll speak to her tonight. Don't worry, I'll make sure she puts her school books back to how they were immediately.'

'Thank you, Mrs Evans. I just wanted to check —'

'And I'm very glad you did. Her father would be furious if he knew!'

My heart started thumping like mad. What was I going to do? I quickly pulled the rest of the books out of my bag, but they all looked as bad. I glanced at my watch. Five minutes before I had to set off for school. Oh my God!

Calm down, Ellie and just think this one through.

Shall I take the labels off?

No, that'd be giving in to Dad.

Shall I keep them on, then?

No, they look awful.

So what then? *I* know – a compromise! I'd unpeel the labels and go back to being Eleanor Stern for just one day, then buy another sheet after school and do them in smaller, neater lettering next time.

So I started picking and scratching at one corner of the label on the history book. It was stuck. I tried another corner but it brought all the surface of the cover with it. I couldn't carry on. I'd completely ruin the book if I did.

Maybe that was just the history book. I tried one of the maths books. No good. The same thing happened. Feeling myself getting into a big state I wrote *Eleanor Evans* in small neat lettering on one of the spare three labels and stuck it over the top of the other one on my history book to try and improve the mess.

It didn't work. The thick black pen from underneath showed through.

So now what? I could feel panic rising up from my stomach.

Keep calm, Eleanor!

I looked at my watch.

Help! I should be setting off now.

Tippex! That's what I needed. I rushed down to the kitchen.

'Where's the Tippex, Mum? It used to be just here.'

She was flying round clearing up. 'I threw it away. It was all caked up round the top.'

'Oh Mum! I need it!'

'I can get some more next time I'm in town. What's so urgent?'

'Oh, nothing!'

Joe and Louise came into the kitchen. 'Come on, Ellie, we're going to be late.'

'Two secs.' I shot back upstairs.

I'd have to get some myself, but did I have enough money? Doubtful. I'd borrow some from Joe. Or Tasha. Or both. I'd buy Tippex and a new sheet of labels straight after school. That still left me with the problem of what to do today.

There was only one thing for it. I'd have to keep the front covers of my books hidden. It wouldn't be all that difficult . . .

. . . would it?

9 THE STATEMENT

It was French first period with Miss Platt. She's one of the young teachers. She's fair and kind, so we all like her. I was sitting next to Tasha. Rachel was just across the aisle from me.

I felt nervous because I was about to take out my French book and I knew I had to be careful that no one, not even Tasha, saw the cover with its embarrassing big black in-your-face label. Just this one day to get through then everything would be fine. I'd have lovely neat little labels tomorrow.

When Miss Platt came into the classroom

everyone glanced up automatically. It's what we all do whenever a teacher comes in to see what kind of mood they're in. It's also interesting, for the girls at least, to see what they're wearing. By the time Miss Platt had got to her desk I'd subtly opened my book.

'What did you get for 4F?' Tasha whispered to me.

I'd completely forgotten that we'd been given homework last week. I like French so I'd done it the same evening it was set, even though we didn't have to hand it in until . . .

Today! *Oh my God, I've got to hand in my book today! What am I going to do?*

For the third time in one morning I had to tell myself to calm down and think.

'*Bonjour, tout le monde,*' said Miss Platt, smiling round the class.

'*Bonjour, Mam'selle Platt,*' we all replied.

If this had been the beginning of year seven instead of the end of year eight we would have probably gone round the class saying what we were called . . . *Je m'appelle Eleanor Evans*.

'Où est le chiffon?' said Miss Platt, looking round. She wasn't testing our understanding of French, she'd genuinely lost the board wiper.

Normally I'd make an effort to help her find it, but today was different. I needed all my concentration to work out how I was going to get out of handing in my French book at the end of the lesson.

My brain was going at three hundred miles an hour, but it suddenly got interrupted by Lucy falling out of her chair. The whole class erupted. I think she'd tried to get out of her place to show Miss Platt where the board wiper was, and she'd been a bit too keen. The boys were laughing their heads off.

'Merci, Lucy!' said Miss Platt.

She carried on talking but I tuned out abruptly. I'd only been distracted by Lucy for about three seconds max, but in that time Tasha had pulled my book towards her to try and subtly copy my answer to number 4F and, big horror, she'd tilted up the cover so she could see to copy.

'Have you changed your name?' Rachel hissed at me. Her mouth was hanging open and she was nodding at my book.

My face went hot and cold at the same time.

Tasha heard what Rachel said and immediately turned to look at the cover. She gasped, 'Did your dad say you could?'

I had about a nano-second to decide whether to tell the truth and feel a complete idiot, or whether to blag it. Something told me that Tasha would disapprove of the truth so blagging won hands down.

'Yeah, after a lot of pestering,' I whispered.

'*Qu'y a-t-il, Eleanor et Natasha?*' Miss Platt's voice made me jump.

She was asking what was the matter. Not in a horrible way – she must have just thought we looked a bit anxious about something.

I was trying not to blush, but it wasn't easy because the two boys from the table in front had turned round.

Robin Cheeseman's eyes went straight to my name label. He was reading it out loud in a puzzled voice. 'Eleanor . . . *Evans*! That's not your name.'

I gave up on trying not to blush. But I had to keep up the pretence. And what's more I had to be convincing.

'It *is*,' I hissed, my heart beating faster.

'So bog off, Cheesy!' said Tasha, springing to my defence.

A few people got out of their places to try and get a better look at my book. I folded my arms across it and put a hard look on my face, even though I was feeling very nervous and embarrassed.

'What's all the fuss about?' asked Miss Platt, dropping her rule about only ever speaking in French during the French lesson.

She was approaching my desk. My heart banged against my ribs as she looked at the cover and frowned. I sat there trying to look cool and calm but feeling stupid and pathetic.

'She's pretending to be Joe's *real* sister!' said Robin, pointing at me and grinning.

'Be quiet, Robin,' said Miss Platt.

'It's 'cos her mum's got married,' said Rachel in a loud, clever voice. 'Eleanor wants her name to be the same as her mum, I expect.'

Lydia Braithwaite, who was the brainiest in the class, whispered to her friend that she thought I was trying to make some kind of statement, doing it that big.

I wished that everyone would shut up. I wanted to wipe the grins off those stupid boys' faces, too.

'I've *changed* my name, if you have to know!' I said quite aggressively. 'I did it by statutory declaration.' I was in such a temper that when I spoke it must have sounded completely convincing.

That shut them up.

Lucy's eyes widened. 'Hey, nice one.'

Most of the others had probably never heard of statutory declaration. It sounded very clever and official. There was a silence. I glared at Robin and his mate and they both turned round to face the front. Rachel leaned back in her chair and Tasha shrank lower in hers. For a moment I truly believed I *had* changed my name. It was a great feeling while it lasted.

'Well . . . congratulations!' said Miss Platt. 'I'm going to have to try and remember not to call you by your . . . original name.' She went back to the front of the class. 'And congratulations to your mum.' By the time she turned round to face us all, she was in control again. '*Alors, on continue . . .*'

So we all got on with the lesson, except for Tasha. I could feel her eyes on me. Although she'd stuck up for me, I knew she wasn't convinced. I guessed she was trying to work out how come I hadn't told her such an important thing before assembly.

My great feeling had gone, leaving me completely churned up.

10 PUSHING THE RIGHT BUTTONS

One lie leads to another. Because of the first lie you have to tell the second one, and because of the second you have to tell the third, and so on.

I was sitting on my bedroom floor surrounded by my books again. Not the French book of course. That had been handed in to Miss Platt. Every time the phone rang my heart stopped until I was quite sure it wasn't the head teacher wanting to talk to Mum. I didn't really think head teachers would make phone calls in the evening, but I couldn't help feeling anxious.

Tasha had quizzed me at break time, and

that's when the second lie had come out.

'No, I *have* changed it, honestly.'

'So how did you get round your dad?'

'I just went on and on about it not being fair and all that.'

'What about Jade and Louise? Surely your parents aren't going to let you change but not them?'

Then came the third. 'They're thinking about letting them change too.'

A quick glance at Tasha told me that she still wasn't convinced. I had to do better.

'Jade's really keen to change now.' (The fourth.) 'She even tried out her new name on the labels that I'd bought. She didn't realise they were for me, you see. That's how come I had to write my own name so big and in such thick pen – to cover hers up!'

I'd tutted and rolled my eyes, but looking back at it now, I don't think Tasha believed me. She'd seemed very quiet for the rest of the day, and when I'd asked if I could borrow some money to buy the Tippex and the new labels she'd handed it over with hardly a word.

'The labels'll look better when I've rewritten them in smaller letters, won't they?' I'd laughed.

'Uh-huh.' But her eyes hadn't met mine.

I had to stop thinking about Tasha now and concentrate on the matter in hand. Right, I said to myself as I started Tippexing. This time I'll make them less obvious.

When I'd Tippexed about five, I reckoned the first one would be dry enough for me to stick a label over it. I was feeling pleased that I hadn't cut corners here. If I'd just tried to write my name over the Tippex it would have gone all wobbly and strange. I wrote out five labels quickly but neatly in small writing with my fine line pen. As I wrote I pretended I'd been doing it for years. It looked much better this time. There was no way Lydia Braithwaite would be able to call *this* a statement. So I carried on and did all the rest.

It was when I was on the last one that there was a knock on my door. I quickly shoved the books, labels and Tippex under the bed. 'Yeah?'

Mum opened the door. 'Can I have a word, please, Eleanor?'

Uh-oh!

She sat down on my bed. I got up and went over to my chest of drawers. I'd left the top of it in a mess, covered with various bath and shower things, sachets of face masks and moisturising cream, pots of body glitter and little trinkets. Good. That gave me something to do. I started to re-arrange everything slowly.

'I had a phone call from school today . . .'

School! Thank goodness I had my back to her so she couldn't see the horror on my face.

I held my breath.

'It was your year eight tutor, Mrs Gordon.'

The way she kept pausing irritated me. It was obvious what was coming. We might as well get on with it.

I swung round and blurted out, 'She wanted to know if I'd changed my name, right?'

'Exactly.' Mum's voice was stressier now. She suddenly bent down and picked up a book that was poking out from under the bed, and looked at it crossly. 'What do you think you're doing, Eleanor? I couldn't believe it when Mrs Gordon told me about your French book.'

I glared at Mum and raised my voice. 'How else am I supposed to get it through to you that I don't want to be called Eleanor Stern any longer? I live *here*. This is my family. I don't want the same name as Dad and Penny. I want the same name as you and Nick.

'Dad isn't too pleased about it, to say the least.'

'You told *Dad*! What did you have to do that for?'

She ignored my question. 'Eleanor, love, you can't just change your name.' Her firm voice was cracking. She was feeling sorry for me, I could tell.

'You can. By statutory declaration.'

An *I'm-older-and-wiser-than-you* look came over Mum's face. She put her hands on her hips. 'And do you know what that involves?'

It was perfectly clear she was about to raise some whopping great problem.

'What?'

'Well, for a start you need consent from both parents, and secondly, it's not exactly cheap.'

And I'd thought it was going to be straightforward. It got me frustrated, and that made me angry. But the thing that made me maddest of all was that Mum still didn't seem to have a clue how important it was to me. She was acting like she agreed with Dad.

I needed to know exactly what the score was here. 'So would *you* let me change if it was only up to you?'

She hesitated. 'Well . . . I'm not sure. I'd certainly consider it.'

This was better. I put on a bit more of a

pleading voice. 'You *do* realise what it's like for me, don't you?'

It was just as though I'd had a choice of ten buttons and I'd chosen the right one. She got up from the bed and gave me a tight hug. 'Yes, I do realise, love. And I wish I could help you.'

That made me feel better. We stayed in the hug for another few seconds then both broke away at the same moment.

'Sorry, Ellie,' said Mum softly.

I managed to smile at her. 'I'm not changing my name back on my school books,' I said, hoping I wasn't pushing my luck. 'I can still be called Eleanor Evans, can't I? There's no harm in it, is there?'

She was frowning deeply. I could practically see her brain whirring away. 'Well . . .'

'As long as I put Stern on my passport and things like that, what's wrong with being Evans for everything else?'

Now she was looking uncomfortable. 'The

trouble is I've told Mrs Gordon that you haven't changed your name, and that it's still Eleanor Stern.'

'Oh Mum! Can't you phone her back tomorrow and explain?'

'It won't be easy to phone back and say something completely different from what I said the day before, love. Mrs Gordon will think I'm a terribly irresponsible parent.'

I had a brainwave. 'Couldn't you just tell her the truth and say that you hadn't realised how important it was for me?' It felt like I was pushing the right button again, if the expression on Mum's face was anything to go by. 'And . . . you could tell her you've decided to let me change it after all.'

The frown was back. 'But that would be lying. And Dad would get to hear about it – we can't expect Jade and Louise to keep it a secret. Just think how upset and angry he'd be.'

So once again it was Dad causing all the

problems and spoiling everything. I was going to look a right idiot if I had to take my lovely new labels off and go back to being Eleanor Stern. Even though most people probably wouldn't say anything nasty to my face, I bet they'd all talk about me behind my back. *Poor Eleanor. She's so sad.*

'I'm not taking the labels off, Mum,' I wailed. 'I'll get the rip taken out of me big time if I do.'

She bit her lip and looked anxiously round the room as if she might find a good solution hiding behind my bin or something. 'OK, I'll speak to Mrs Gordon tomorrow and I'll try and explain everything. I'll ask her if you can keep the labels there till the end of term, as there isn't long to go. Next term you'll be in a brand new year and we can start all over again. People will have forgotten about it. And if they *do* happen to remember you can say it was *your* decision to go back to Stern.'

She was looking at me with a hopeful expression on her face. I had to think this one through carefully.

'So if I keep the labels till the end of term that means I get to be called Eleanor Evans till then, yeah?'

I was beginning to feel excited because surely by the end of term everyone would have got so much into the habit of calling me by my new name, that it would be impossible to go back to the other one. Mum and maybe even Dad would have got used to it by then too, and I'd be allowed to change it officially. Permanently. This was beginning to work out perfectly.

Mum sighed a big sigh and I knew then that it wasn't quite as perfect as I'd thought. 'Look, I'll ask Mrs Gordon to have a word with the other teachers so they don't raise their eyebrows or anything when they see your books or hear any of the pupils referring to you by that name. But that's all I can do, I'm afraid, love. I can't ask the teachers to call you by that name when it simply isn't your name.' She raised her chin and looked me in the eyes. 'And that's that.'

It wasn't enough. I'd still have to suffer hearing the name Eleanor Stern at every registration. And then people would say '*It's not Eleanor Stern, it's Eleanor Evans, Miss,*' and Mrs Gordon would wear that same *I'm-older-and-wiser-than-you* look and come out with some clever reason why we were sticking with Stern for the time being. Just thinking about it made me start to go red. And that made me angry. It was all Dad's fault.

In a flash I decided something important. I'd already planned not to go over to Dad's any more, but now I had a small change to make to the plan. I wouldn't go over to Dad's *until he agreed that I could change my name.*

'OK, whatever,' I said, making my voice all light and carefree.

A suspicious look came over Mum's face,

then changed into a worried one. She didn't understand why I seemed so cool all of a sudden.

The power I felt reminded me of a time when I'd been playing a card game called Trumps with Louise, Mum, Nick and Joe. Everyone had been trying to work out who'd got the ace of trumps – the best card of all. I'd not given away that it was me, just joined in with the guessing to put them off the scent. Then when I finally played it and won the game, everyone had gasped and said, 'Ellie! You had it all the time! You clever thing!'

11 AN ODD WEEKEND

On Friday morning I woke up in a sweat. I'd been dreaming that Mrs Gordon had called the register over a loudspeaker, which boomed out over the whole town. And Dad had been shopping in the high street at the time so when he heard her say 'Eleanor Evans' he went crazy and roared up to school on a motorbike, then rampaged round the corridors like a mad bull, looking for her. When he finally found her hiding behind a wastepaper bin, he wrapped her up in a big white sheet and wrote *Eleanor Stern* in huge black letters all over it.

The dream had seemed so realistic. And it wouldn't leave me.

I was dreading registration.

'Morning, everyone,' smiled Mrs Gordon as she came into the classroom. She glanced round at us and spotted the big badge that Charlotte was wearing. 'Ooh, Charlotte! Happy birthday!'

Charlotte's best friend Amy started singing 'Happy birthday to you . . .' and everyone joined in, except the boys, who groaned, and waited with over-the-top bored looks on their faces for us to finish. And with every word I sang I felt a bit more nervous about what was to come any minute now.

'Have a nice day, Charlotte,' smiled Mrs Gordon. Then she opened her register and began. 'Rebecca?'

'Yes, Miss.'

'Tom?'

'Yes, Miss.'

That's when I clicked. Of course! She never says our surnames when she calls the register. I needn't have worried at all. The feeling of relief was massive. Until . . .

I came back to the here and now with a start at the sound of Robin Cheeseman's voice. 'Did you know Eleanor's changed her name, Miss?'

'I don't think that's got anything whatsoever to do with you, Robin,' said Mrs Gordon briskly.

I lowered my eyes. It was embarrassing, but at least she wasn't denying it. It could have been worse.

Mum didn't get into a stress when I said I wasn't going to Dad's with Jade and Louise. She'd probably not been expecting me to go as I'd been there so recently. Just wait till next time though, and the one after that! Then everyone'd realise I meant business.

On Sunday Joe and I went with Mum and Nick to a town nearby where they were holding a fair. Joe and I saw quite a few people from school and I left him chucking wet sponges at people pretending to be in the stocks like in the Middle Ages, while I went off with Lucy and one or two others. We got our hair braided and had our fortunes told. Gipsy Gisella didn't give me any clues about what was going to happen about my name and everything, but she did say I was going to get married in my twenties and have three children.

When we got back Dad was already parked outside the house. I made a point of not bothering to even look in his direction as I went up the front path.

'Where've you been?' asked Jade, tumbling out of the car and racing after me.

'To Heatherington,' said Mum.

'To a fair,' I added over my shoulder.

Mum pursed her lips. I knew I was stirring things up, making Jade wish she'd been with us, but it was the only way I could get back at Dad.

Louise waved Dad off then caught us up. 'We've had a brilliant time,' she said, looking at Jade pointedly. 'Haven't we, Jade?'

'It was a bit boring,' said Jade. 'Max and Jamie were at their friend's house.'

Mum sounded surprised. 'Oh, right.'

Louise looked embarrassed. 'It wasn't boring.' She turned to Jade. 'You enjoyed baking, didn't you?'

'Not with Dad helping. He didn't know what to do.'

'The cakes were lovely in the end though, weren't they?'

Jade nodded, but she was looking round for Telly, her cat, and I could tell she hadn't really been very impressed with the baking.

'Didn't Penny help with the cakes?' asked Mum.

'She was ill,' said Jade. 'In bed with a very bad tummy ache.'

Louise didn't say anything.

'Oh dear, poor Penny,' said Mum.

'And we weren't allowed to see her. Not even to give her a cup of tea or anything,' Jade carried on grumpily.

'Oh dear,' Mum repeated, frowning.

Then Louise looked daggers at me as though I'd been the one to make Penny have a tummy ache.

How unfair was *that*?

12 THE TURNING POINT

On Monday evening we all ate together as usual, except Jade. Jade can't last out till seven o'clock and anyway it's her bedtime. She was watching telly in the other room in her dressing gown and the rest of us were eating cheesy pasta when the phone rang. Mum answered it.

She sounded rather odd. 'Well, we're just eating actually. Shall I ask her to phone you back?' There was a pause then she said, 'Yes, all right. Hang on.' She covered the mouthpiece. 'It's Dad. He wants a word with you, Eleanor.'

I bet I knew what *that* was about. Dad

wanted to give me a big lecture on how I wasn't allowed to change my name, and I wanted to hear it about as much as I wanted double detention.

'This'll go cold,' I told Mum, eating another mouthful of pasta.

'*I'll* speak to him,' said Louise, jumping up.

Mum hesitated then handed her the phone.

Louise always shows every single emotion on her face when she talks on the phone. It's as though she thinks that if she exaggerates a smile or a sad look, the person on the other end might develop X-ray eyes and be able to see it. Right now her eyes were nearly popping out of her head and she was gesticulating with the hand that wasn't holding the phone.

'Yes . . . We had double maths and it was one of those speed tests. We swapped papers to mark them. I had to mark Becky Anderson's. She got six out of ten. I got seven.' (*Pause while he spoke and she kept grinning.*) 'She's in the other room watching telly in her dressing gown because she's had a bath.' (*Brief pause while Louise eyed up my plate. I guessed she'd been asked to report back about how I was getting on, so I deliberately helped myself to some more pasta.*) 'She's still got quite a bit on her plate, Dad . . .' (*The beam dropped on to the floor and Louise's eyes went all sad.*) 'Yeah, OK. Is Penny better?' (*Another pause. The sad eyes didn't change.*) 'Say hello from me and give her my love . . . and Jade's and Eleanor's, of course, and give her a big hug from me . . . and from Jade and Eleanor . . .' (*The tops of her cheeks were bright pink.*) 'Only make sure you don't hug too tight!' (*Back came the beam. Dad must have appreciated the joke.*) 'Yeah . . . I'll tell her . . . Yeah . . . OK . . . lots of love . . . Byeeeeeee!'

She came back to her place and started piling more pasta on her plate. Then she gave me a bit of a cross look. 'You've got to ring Dad when you've finished.'

'Hey! Leave enough for me!' said Joe,

giving the pasta bowl a worried look.

'Whoops! Sorry.'

'There's more,' said Mum, flapping her hand vaguely in the direction of the cooker. She was gazing at the salt and pepper, clearly thinking about something else entirely.

I wondered whether I could get away with not phoning. Mum was wrapped up in her own thoughts, and anyway she'd be going to read Jade a story very soon. Nick had finished his meal and was reaching for the paper. Joe wouldn't give the phone call another thought because he nearly always minded his own business. That just left Louise, and as long as she finished eating before me and left the table first, she'd probably forget about it. Sorted. All I had to do was eat really slowly.

The plan would have worked if it hadn't been for Jade. I was in the middle of chewing the smallest mouthful known to man when she burst in.

'Guess what!'

'What?' Louise and I asked at the same time.

Jade's eyes were massive as she began to tell us what she'd been watching. 'The man did find them in the end and they promised never ever to run away again. And the boy had big patches of blood on his leg.'

It was so tempting to laugh, because we'd no idea what she was on about, but whatever programme it was, had obviously had a big effect on her. 'Well, that sounds like a happy ending,' said Mum absent-mindedly.

'Apart from the blood,' Nick pointed out.

'D'you mind not talking about blood?' said Joe, pulling a face. 'Some of us are still eating.'

'Sorry,' said Jade. She dropped her voice to a whisper. 'Rosie says it's tomato ketchup really but it's not. It's proper blood. I could tell.'

'Well, thanks for that,' said Joe.

'Time for bed, I think,' said Mum, getting up.

They were almost out of the door when Jade

swung round and said, 'Who was on the phone?'

'Oh yes,' said Mum, turning round and practically wagging her finger at me. 'Don't forget to phone Dad back the moment you've finished, all right?'

I gave something resembling a nod, then carried on eating. There was a pause before the door shut. I bet Mum had given Nick a look to say *Make sure she does, can you*?

My pasta was practically cold, I'd been eating so slowly, so I decided to give up on it. I asked if I could leave the table and Nick said, 'Yes, go and give your dad a quick ring, eh?' He was holding out the phone which I took reluctantly. I'd been right about that look.

'OK.'

He would assume I was going to phone from my room, but as I went upstairs I decided not to bother. I'd pretend I'd got so involved with my homework that I'd forgotten all about phoning.

I started reading a brilliant book that Tasha

had given me and really did forget about the phone until it suddenly rang loudly right in my ear, making me jump. There was only one other phone in the house and that was in Mum and Nick's room. They'd be cross if they had to come rushing upstairs because I was ignoring it, so I was stuck. I had to answer it.

'Hello.'

'Hello, Ellie. It's Dad.'

Groan!

I decided to play it cool. 'Hi.'

'Had a good day?' I could tell from his voice that he was trying to butter me up.

'Not particularly, no.'

'Oh . . . right. School not so good, then?'

'School was fine.'

I knew I was being horrible, but how else was I supposed to let him know how I felt?

'I was wondering, Ellie, would you like to meet up in town at the Caffé Uno? Just you and me? For a chat?'

He'd really surprised me. Caffé Uno. Just him and me. It sounded quite grown up. And come to think about it, he didn't seem at all cross. I suddenly clicked. Dad had finally realised I was a teenager and it was about time he treated me like one. I guessed he was also feeling pretty guilty about not letting me change my name. This Caffé Uno thing was his way of showing me how he'd changed. And 'a chat' – great! He probably wanted to tell me it was all right about my name, after all.

'Yes, OK. When?'

'What about tomorrow? I've got an appointment in town at three o'clock. I could meet you after that. If you catch the bus from school, what time can you be there?'

'Er . . . four-ish.'

'That's fine then. I'll see you tomorrow.'

I skipped downstairs with the phone, feeling a zillion times better than I had done an hour before.

13 CAFFÉ UNO

I felt quite grown up walking into Caffé Uno on my own, and didn't mind at all that Dad wasn't there. I told the waitress I was waiting for someone, and she said she'd come back to take our order when he appeared.

I only had to wait about three minutes.

'Sorry, Ellie. The meeting went on a bit longer than I'd expected and I couldn't get away.'

'That's all right.'

The waitress came straight over.

'We'll have a pot of tea for two, please. And what would you like to eat, Ellie?'

'Can I have a toasted teacake?'

'Sure. Anything else?'

I shook my head.

'Two toasted teacakes then, thanks.' He took his jacket off and asked me if I'd had a good day.

'Yeah, fine.' I didn't want to waste time talking about boring things. 'Dad?'

'Yes.'

'You know . . . this thing about my name?'

A shadow passed over his face. 'Uh-huh.'

'Well, I *have* thought it through, you know.'

'Have you?'

'Yes, and lots of people do it.'

'Do they?'

He was drumming his fingers on the table. 'Look, can we talk about something else for a few minutes?'

What?

'But I want to talk about this. It's very important to me, Dad.'

He looked away and back again. 'OK, well,

let's just wait for the tea to arrive then.' He tried to hide a sigh. 'How's your singing going? You've not mentioned that in a while. Doing any stuff with Joe these days?'

Oh p-lease! This was just as bad as usual. Dad was talking to me in that false way that irritates me so much. Fortunately I didn't have to answer because the waitress appeared with our tea and teacakes. She seemed to take ages putting everything from her tray on to the table, and I didn't want to talk until she'd finished. Dad obviously didn't want to either, so we sat in silence and watched her every move. As she put down the sugar bowl I suddenly remembered something Tasha had pointed out.

The moment we were on our own again I started gabbling. 'Look, I know you don't like the idea of me changing my name, but I'll be changing it anyway when I get married and you won't mind about that, will you? So what's the difference?'

I sat back, feeling quite pleased with my argument.

He took a big gulp of tea then said, 'Exactly.'

'What?'

'Well, when do you imagine you'll get married?'

'I dunno.'

He sighed. 'Roughly?'

I decided to say the earliest possible time I could think of, to make the point that it was really hardly any different changing my name now from changing it in a very few years' time.

'Say I got married when I was . . . twenty one. That's only eight years.'

'Exactly. There's no point in changing it if you're only going to be changing it again in eight years.'

I couldn't believe how he'd twisted it. 'But what if I don't get married till I'm in my thirties – or *never*?'

He closed his eyes and opened them again slowly. 'I think you're missing the point, Ellie.'

'No, Dad, *you're* the one who's missing the point.'

He looked round then spoke quietly. 'Keep your voice down.'

I leaned forwards and spoke in a fierce whisper because I didn't care how cross he got any more. It wasn't like I was stuck at his house. I could just walk out of Caffé Uno, couldn't I?

'You don't know what it's like living in a family where the two grown-ups have got a different name from you. And now Mum's having a baby in October . . .' I glanced at him.

He nodded. 'Louise said.' Then he sat back in his chair and breathed out slowly.

This wasn't how Dad normally acted. Why weren't the muscles in his jaw tightening up like they always did when he got cross? And there was something else missing too. What was it?

No time to think about that now, Ellie. Just keep talking.

'So then there'll be more Evanses than Sterns

in the house, and that'll make it even worse.'

Maybe I should have stopped then and let him speak, but I went plunging on. 'Mum doesn't mind me changing at all. She said it was fine with her. She completely understands, you see.'

'Well she would, wouldn't she?'

I'd never heard him talk like this. And I'd never seen him look like this either. His eyes were all blank.

'Wh-what do you mean?'

He shook his head and stared into his empty cup as though he was reading the tea leaves.

There was a long pause then he spoke in a low voice, but it wasn't an answer to my question. 'OK, then. If it's so important to you, you might as well go ahead and do it.'

Just like that? I couldn't believe my ears.

'Are you sure?'

He nodded.

'Hello, Jim!' A man in a suit had appeared at

our table. 'So this is where you escaped to, is it?' He slapped Dad on the back.

'Hello, Chris,' Dad said in a tight voice. 'This is my daughter Ellie. This is Chris, Ellie. He was at the meeting just now.'

'Pleased to meet you,' said the man, giving me a vague smile. He looked round. 'I'm supposed to be meeting Gary. Doesn't seem to be here yet. I'll go and grab a table anyway.'

He went, and I felt like going too because if I stayed, there was always the risk that Dad might change his mind. Anyway, he was obviously fed up about my decision, so it would be embarrassing trying to have a normal conversation now.

'*I'd* better go too, actually, Dad. I've got to take my books back to the library before it closes.'

He nodded slowly, staring at the sugar bowl, then dragged his eyes over to me and said, 'Get your mum to give me a ring. We'll have to have a chat about which solicitor we want to use and so on.'

Wow! He really *did* mean business.

'Yes, OK. I'll tell her to phone you tonight.'

I hurried out of Caffé Uno, still puzzling about Dad and what was different about him.

14 THE SEARCHLIGHT

The moment Mum walked through the door with Jade I told her the news. 'Guess what? Dad's agreed!'

'What?' said Jade. 'A greed . . . y pig?'

Mum looked suddenly tired. 'Go and change into your shorts and blue T-shirt, Jade, and bring that mucky dress down for the wash.'

Jade did as she was told. As soon as she'd gone Mum turned to me. 'What do you mean?'

'Well, I met him in Caffé Uno, like we arranged, and I went on about changing my name and he suddenly agreed. He wants you to phone him to sort out the solicitor.'

Mum was staring at me in open-mouthed shock.

'It's good, isn't it?' I said, giving her a big smile.

She sat down at the kitchen table. 'I'm . . . really amazed. I mean . . . what did you say to him?'

'Just that it was really bad living with two grown-ups who didn't have the same name as you . . . and all that stuff.' I wanted to stop talking about it, and get on with making it happen. 'So can you phone him, Mum?'

Still staring straight ahead in disbelief, she nodded.

At eight-thirty there was a knock on my bedroom door and Mum came in.

'Have you phoned Dad? Is it sorted?' I started gabbling. 'When are we going to the solicitor's?'

Mum was about to answer when Louise appeared. Bad timing.

'I thought I heard you say "'Bye, Jim,"' she said to Mum, her face a mixture of curiosity and worry. 'Were you talking to Dad?'

'Yes.'

Mum only ever has long phone calls with Dad if it's something important to do with us lot, so I suppose it was no wonder Louise was anxious. But right now it was bugging me badly that she was hanging around.

She gave Mum an exasperated look. 'Why didn't you tell me you were phoning Dad? *I* wanted to talk to him.'

'Did you?' said Mum in a vague, thin voice I didn't recognise.

'Yes, I wanted to ask if I could go over there again this weekend.'

Louise was really winding me up, going on about spending yet another weekend at Dad's.

I turned on her. 'What for? You've been there for the last two weekends. Isn't that enough?'

Her sweet round face suddenly went pointed

and hard. 'I'm trying to make up for *you*, that's why!' She turned to Mum, her cheeks bright red and her eyes flashing angrily. 'Eleanor's horrible to Dad and Penny. She didn't even act properly happy when they told us that Penny —'

'Shut up!' I interrupted, in my own temper now. 'That's supposed to be a secret!'

'It's . . . OK,' said Mum, in that same weak voice. 'I've heard from Dad.'

Louise didn't wait another second. She started gabbling in a big temper. 'Well, you should have seen her, Mum. She acted like she didn't care about the baby. And I feel sorry for them. *And* I feel sorry for the poor baby. Eleanor's not interested in it and Jade's not interested in *any* babies — she says they're boring because they don't do anything or say anything. And that means that their poor little baby won't have any sisters except me to love it . . .'

She stopped abruptly, and I saw her red cheeks go mottled and a frown gather on her face.

She was looking at Mum. I followed her gaze.

No wonder Louise was a bit fazed. Mum's face was very still.

'What?' asked Louise in a small voice.

Mum replied in scarcely more than a whisper. 'There's some bad news . . .' I felt my whole body tense up. 'Penny's had a miscarriage. I'm afraid she's lost the baby. Dad's just told me.'

Louise's face crumpled, and a second later she let out a loud wailing cry and bolted out of the room.

As Mum turned to follow her out, she spoke to me in a flat voice. 'That's what Dad wanted to tell you in Caffé Uno.'

Her words winded me more than a kick in the stomach. I collapsed on my bed, and felt the inside of my body crumpling just like Louise's face had done. From the other side of the wall I could hear fast guitar-playing. Joe was playing his favourite CD. It sounded to my fuzzy mind like it was coming from the other end of a tunnel. I replayed the conversation I'd had in Caffé Uno with Dad. What a stupid idiot I'd been! Stupid and selfish and thoughtless. I couldn't bear to think about it. I broke down in tears and rolled on to my stomach to stifle my sobs so Joe wouldn't hear me. I could hardly breathe but I kept my face pressed into the pillow.

A moment later I felt a hand on my head. I knew it was Mum. I turned my face the tiniest bit so I could speak through my tears.

'That's why Dad said it was OK for me to change my name, wasn't it? Because it's like nothing compared to losing a little baby, is it?'

Mum started stroking my hair. Her voice was strong again now. 'I don't think he had the energy to argue any more. He told me that he used to think that if you still had his name it would give him some kind of hold over you. But then he suddenly realised in the café that actually he had very little hold over you. You were getting older and making up your own mind about things, and eventually he wouldn't have any hold at all. So he decided that there was no point in sticking out over a name – because actually the name itself didn't make any difference to anything.'

Mum's words only made me feel sadder and more confused than ever. I didn't want her sitting there, stroking my hair and telling me these things. It was too hard to listen to. I shook her hand off and she got up. A moment later I heard my bedroom door closing.

I cried and cried and cried then because I hadn't really wanted her to go. I didn't even care that Joe must have been able to hear me. In fact I wanted him to hear. I wanted him to come in and say something to make it better. But a part of me was scared in case he said something that made it worse. And all the time my head felt hotter and hotter and heavier and heavier, full of thoughts that were all mangled up because they'd been tossed around so much. If only I could straighten them out and make them settle down and stop spinning and banging against each other. I kicked my legs in frustration and anger, pummelling the bed noisily.

So I never heard the bedroom door open.

'What's the matter, Eleanor?'

Joe's shaky voice made me jump. I stopped kicking, and lay there rigid and silent for a second, but then my crying came back in full force. I couldn't stop it.

'Do you want me to go away?'

Yes I do, because if you stay I'll have to try and explain what's the matter and I can't.

No, I don't because I feel so lonely.

I couldn't even answer a simple question any more. A new wave of crying came over me. The biggest, noisiest one of all. It went on and on and on until I was exhausted and just lay there, still and silent. I turned my face to the side and stared at the wallpaper. This used to be Louise's room before Joe moved in with us. I'd let him have my room, and Louise had let me have hers. We hadn't got round to changing her wallpaper. It had pink hearts all over it that looked as though they were lit up. When you peered closely at just one heart, like I was doing, you could see how the artist had made the light effect by dabbing on a darker bit at the bottom and a pale yellowy triangular bit near the top. It took the magic out of the hearts, seeing them so close up.

'I'll go then, shall I?'

I shot up. His voice had given me a shock. I thought he'd already gone. Then I remembered that I'd got a horrible puffy face, and quickly flopped back, turning away. There was a silence. I started to panic. He *would* go if I didn't say something else quickly and I didn't want to drive another person away.

I knew my voice was shaking, but I couldn't do anything about it. 'If you look at one of these hearts on the wallpaper from really close up, you can see how the artist has made it look like it's lit up.'

There was a pause. I guessed he was probably studying one of them. Joe's really into art. It would probably be safe to turn my head.

I was right. He was by the door, his nose about two centimetres away from the wallpaper.

'I heard you and Louise yelling at each other. What was that about?'

I did one of those juddery sobs that you do when you've been really crying and your breathing hasn't gone back to normal. I felt stupid. It just came out.

'You don't have to tell me if you don't want to.' He opened the door and I started panicking again.

'Louise is cross with me because I'm not interested in going over to Dad's . . . and she *is*.' I stopped. That was all I could manage.

'So why does that make her cross?'

'Because she thinks I ought to care more about Dad and the baby and everything. Only there isn't going to be a baby now.' I bit my lip. I didn't want to start crying again. It hurt too much.

'Yeah. Sylvia said. Do you feel guilty then?'

'I don't know.' I did another of those shuddery breaths which turned into a big sigh.

Joe was staring at the carpet. 'It's funny about babies, isn't it? Like when Sylvia and Dad told us about Sylvia being pregnant, I felt really pleased, 'cos – you know, I've only got Dad and I thought . . . that'll make, like, three of us.'

New tears welled up in my eyes. I couldn't bear to hear my tough stepbrother talking like this. I wished I could think of something to say to make him feel better. 'You've got us three stepsisters,' I said quietly.

'Yeah, I know. But if your mum and my dad ever split up it'd just be me and Dad again 'cos – you know, this is like one of those families you can chop right down the middle, and it's obvious that you lot'd go with your mum and I'd go with Dad. Only now, with the baby . . .'

I waited. He was flexing his fingers and studying them intently at the same time. I'd hardly ever heard Joe say so much all in one go '. . . there'll be something to stop the split being that easy, won't there?' He suddenly looked up and gave me a bit of an embarrassed smile. 'So I don't have to worry about that one any more.'

I tried to swallow but I couldn't. The lump in my throat was too big. Why had I cared so much about cutting people out of my life when Joe was scared of finding himself back with just one person? He'd got a *real* worry. I'd just got . . . an obsession. Yes, that was it. I'd been completely obsessed.

The feeling that came over me at that moment was incredible, like a powerful force that was shining a searchlight into my mind, seeking out the rotten remains of my pathetic thoughts and pulling them out with a great big pair of tweezers.

I attempted a reassuring smile for Joe but it probably came out like a terrible grimace because my mouth was wobbling about so much, I was in such a shaky state. I concentrated on my eyes and put all my feelings in them.

A look of relief came over his face. I wasn't sure whether it was because he was glad I'd got over that crying fit at last, or whether he was relieved to have told someone his worry.

The moment was past though. And I guess I'll never know.

15 THE BIG BLURRY PICTURE

I couldn't stop thinking about Dad. I went through lesson after lesson the next day, taking in absolutely nothing because my mind was full up with my own thoughts. At the end of double English, when Tasha and I were packing away, she suddenly said, 'What's up, Ell? It's like you're on another planet today.'

She was looking at me with big kind eyes. I suddenly wanted to feel that tightening of our friendship bond. Things hadn't really been the same since last Thursday when she'd lent me the money for the Tippex.

So we stayed in the English room and I spilled out everything. The more I talked, the more I didn't understand myself. 'I feel so stupid, Tasha. Fancy being obsessed with getting Dad and Penny and the twins out of my life and changing my name when poor Joe's been worrying about how bad it would be if Nick and Mum ever split up.'

'I bet you wish you could go over to your dad's right now, don't you?'

It was lovely having a best friend who understood me so well.

'Yeah. I'm going to phone him tonight and say I'll come with Louise at the weekend.' Then I had another thought – an even better one. 'Hey, maybe I could go this evening!'

Tasha's eyes lit up but only for a second. 'That's what *I* was thinking!'

'Are *you* OK, Tash?'

She sighed and her eyes went dull. 'It's only Mum and Dad arguing again . . .'

'Poor you. I'm always going on about my problems and forgetting about you. Sorry, Tash.'

'It's OK. It's just the same old problem as usual. Only . . .'

She stopped and bit her lip.

'What?'

'Well, I'm not sure if you'll want to hear this, but Mum told me something last night.'

'What?'

'Your mum *did* phone up and ask if you could stay over with us while your mum and Nick were away.'

A coldness came over me. 'She *did*?'

'Yeah, and Mum explained to your mum about how she and Dad had got big problems, and told her it wouldn't be fair on you having to stay in a house full of arguments and bad atmosphere. And your mum said not to worry at all, she'd sort something else out.'

I found it difficult to swallow. That was something else that I'd blamed on Dad that wasn't his fault at all. Then there was Mum. She'd obviously tried to be nice to Tasha's parents by not telling me the truth about why I couldn't stay there. It looked like I'd got everything wrong. I felt such an idiot.

The one day I was desperate for Mum to get back from work early, she was late. Jade came in just in front of her, singing a pop song loudly. Fortunately she went straight through to the other room.

'Sorry I'm late, love, I was having a cup of tea with Diane.'

'It's OK. Mum?'

She looked at me carefully. 'Yes?'

I felt my cheeks getting hotter, but decided to plunge on before I lost my nerve. 'I know you've only just got back from work and everything, but could you take me over to Dad's?'

'To Dad's?' She looked gobsmacked.

'I want to say sorry about the baby. I was

thinking that maybe if you took me there, Dad'd bring me back.'

'It's a lovely idea, Ellie. But have you actually phoned Dad? It might not be a good time for them.'

My heart was thumping as I tapped in the number. I suddenly felt so embarrassed about everything. He answered it on the fifth ring.

'Hello?' His voice was brisk.

I gulped. 'It's Ellie.'

There was a tiny silence then he said, 'Hello, Ellie,' in a strange voice – half pleased, half wary. 'How's it going?'

'I was wondering if I could come over actually.'

'Yes, of course. Louise is coming, you know.'

'No, I didn't mean at the weekend, I meant now.'

'Oh, right.'

'Mum says she'll bring me.'

'Great! Come over, yes. I'll tell Penny you're on your way. The twins'll be pleased to see you.'

When we'd rung off, Mum left Joe and Louise in charge of Jade, and told them she'd be back in twenty-five minutes. Louise looked as though she was about to protest but I saw Mum give her a little shake of the head, and she kept quiet.

It was on Mum's third attempt at getting the car started that my heart began to sink. There didn't seem to be any life at all in the engine. Joe came out and made a couple of suggestions. We even phoned Nick on his mobile because he was working late again, but when Mum described the problem, he just said it didn't sound too good and that he'd take a look the next day.

Mum put her hand on my shoulder. 'You'd better phone Dad and explain, love. We'll try and get something sorted out for tomorrow evening.'

But when I phoned Dad he immediately offered to come and pick me up.

My spirits soared and I went straight to the window to look out for him, even though I knew there was no way he could get to us in under twelve minutes.

The very second his car came round the corner I belted out of the front door calling over my shoulder, 'See you later!'

But Mum rushed out after me and Dad rolled down his window.

'This is for you and Penny,' she said, handing Dad a pale green envelope.

Dad gave her a weak kind of smile as he thanked her and I got into the passenger seat. We were about to set off when Jade came belting out of the house. 'Daddy! Daddy! Why's Ellie going to your house and not me? I want to go too.'

I crossed my fingers that Mum would tell her she wasn't allowed, but Jade was already opening the back door of the car.

Something must have caught Dad's eye in the house. 'Oh dear, there's Louise.'

I looked up to see Louise waving sadly from

her bedroom window. She obviously thought Jade had been allowed to come but she hadn't.

Mum saw her too. 'Look,' she said to Dad. 'I've got an idea. Why don't you come in and have a cup of tea with us? Then everyone'll get to see you.'

Dad was frowning. He wasn't sure.

Neither was I. 'But I wanted to see *Penny*, Mum.'

'Yeah, phone Penny!' said Jade, leaning forward between the front seats of the car. 'She can come too!'

Dad turned round and smiled. 'Penny can't leave the twins,' he said.

'She could bring them, couldn't she, Mum?' said Jade, eyes sparkling.

'Not really . . .' Dad began, looking a bit embarrassed. Then he turned to me. 'Maybe you could pop over tomorrow, Ellie, and I'll just stay for a quick cup of tea now.'

Mum must have realised how disappointed I

was. 'Maybe Penny's not feeling well enough yet?' Mum asked Dad carefully.

'Oh, she's much better now,' said Dad.

'Look, Daddy, *you* go and get Penny and Max and Jamie and we'll wait for you here,' said Jade rather bossily as she clambered out of the car. 'Mum'll phone Penny, OK?'

She turned her palms up as if to say, *It's so easy, I don't know why you grown-ups can't work it out for yourselves!*

Mum smiled and nodded at Dad. 'That's fine by me.'

'I'll come with you, Dad,' I said.

And luckily Dad pulled away before Jade got any ideas.

Neither Dad nor I spoke for a minute or two, then we both spoke at once.

'I'm sorry about –'

'So how was your –'

We both laughed a bit nervously.

'I was going to say I'm really sorry about

Penny having a miscarriage.'

He kept his eyes on the road and nodded slowly. 'Maybe she'll get pregnant again . . . soon.'

'Yes, I'm sure she will. I mean, I hope she does.'

We were silent again. I wanted to say more, much more, but I couldn't seem to be able to find the right words.

Just keep talking, Ellie. Say anything.

'Do you think Penny'll want to come over to our house?'

'It depends how she feels.'

'But will she mind Mum phoning her? Mightn't she think it's a bit kind of weird?'

He took his eyes of the road for a second to look at me. 'What about you? Do *you* think it's a bit weird?'

It was true, I certainly would have found it weird a couple of days ago – in fact more than weird, absolutely terrible. But what did I think now? I tried to untangle my thoughts.

'I'm not too sure,' I replied hesitantly.

He smiled then, and drove a bit faster. '*Not sure* will do for now.'

I wanted to say sorry about how I'd been in Caffé Uno, but Dad started telling me a funny story about the man called Chris who we'd seen in there, and it went on for ages. I wasn't really concentrating properly on what he was saying because I was trying to work out what was different about him. It was the same thing as I'd noticed in Caffé Uno. Something was missing, but I still couldn't tell what.

It wasn't until we pulled up outside his house that it hit me.

'Wait here,' he said. 'I won't be a sec . . .'

I could only nod. The old Dad would have said, *You wait here, Ellie, and I'll round up the troops* or something false-sounding like that. But this was a different Dad. There was no falseness. The barrier between us had gone. *That's* what was missing.

As he went into the house I got in the back, feeling nervous about seeing Penny. Then I noticed that Dad had left Mum's card in the front so I reached forward for it. I'd give Penny the card as soon as she got in the car and that would make it less embarrassing.

But when five minutes had gone by and there was no sign of them at all, my nervousness turned to anxiety. Maybe this new dad wasn't interested in me any more and had forgotten that I was outside his house in the car.

Then they suddenly emerged and the relief was enormous, and all mixed up with a new burst of nervousness. I felt myself shrinking into the corner as the twins piled in, talking quickly in high-pitched voices about how Jamie had tipped his glass of water over and wet his T-shirt and jeans so he'd had to change. They thought it was hilarious because most of the water had settled in his lap and Max said it looked like he'd done a wee.

The moment they stopped talking and giggling I handed the card to Penny. 'This is from Mum. She didn't know she was going to see you herself, you see.'

'Oh, that's sweet of her,' said Penny, but I noticed she didn't open it.

I wanted to say that I was sorry, only I didn't think I ought to with Jamie and Max there. So I said it inside my head as a sort of preparation. But then I realised that it would be impossible to say it this evening, because there would be so many people about. How would I ever be able to talk in private with Dad and Penny? I'd just have to wait till tomorrow.

'Hello, everybody!' yelled Jade, coming out of the front door like a stone from a catapult as we pulled up.

The twins undid their seat belts and scrambled out of the car.

I was alone with Penny and Dad, and I knew I couldn't wait till tomorrow to say what I had to say because tomorrow would be too late.

Swarms of butterflies seemed to have invaded my stomach.

Just speak, Ellie. 'Um . . . can I tell you something?'

Penny and Dad both turned round, looking alarmed.

'I . . . I . . .' It was too big to explain. I didn't know where to begin. I took a deep breath and tried again. 'I . . .'

Penny twisted round even more so she could reach to put a hand on my knee. 'We know you're upset, Ellie. Your mum told us. We think we understand a bit what you're feeling.'

'No, no you don't!' I said. 'I . . . I . . .' But still the words wouldn't come. Then out of the corner of my eye I saw Mum walking down the drive very slowly towards us. Her head was tipped to one side as though she wanted to check that we were all right. Louise was at her side, looking anxious and behind them was Joe, hands in pockets, and Nick, who'd obviously got home earlier than he'd thought he was going to. It was like a procession, and bringing up the rear was Jade, sitting in a King's carry on the twins' hands.

I'll never forget this picture of my big, mixed-up family coming down to meet me and Dad and Penny. The sight of them like this made the two frames collapse inside my head, so there was only a blur left where the family overlaps were all smudged. It seemed as though the picture was going out of focus, but it wasn't. It was just that everyone was too close to the car now for me to see properly.

'I'm not changing my name,' I said softly.

Dad and Penny both broke into big smiles.

I'd said the most important thing. And I'd only just been in time because Jade had overtaken everyone and was opening Dad's door for him.

'Come on, you lazy people!' she said.

I got out of the car and went to walk to the house next to Louise. She was sucking her cheeks in.

'Are you all right?' I whispered.

She nodded but she looked anxious.

'Don't worry about me, Lou, I've just been going through a stupid phase,' I said.

'It was like you weren't the same Ellie,' she said quietly.

'Sorry.' It was all I could think of saying. 'I'm back now.'

Her eyes went all shiny as she let her cheeks out.

I turned round. Mum and Penny were talking in low voices, their heads close together. Dad and Nick were just ahead of them, discussing Mum's car engine. In front of me Max and Jade were reciting a poem loudly and Jamie had tucked his hand into Joe's.

And I was in the middle. Right in the middle of this lovely big blurry family picture.

The two frames had turned into one.

Inside me, the bubbles were bursting, as they had done so often recently. But it wasn't anger that swished and surged around my body. It was something else.

Something much closer to happiness.

Collect the links in the step-chain . . .

 1. To see her dad, Sarah has to stay with the woman who wrecked her family. Will she do it? Find out in *One Mum Too Many!*

 2. Ollie thinks a holiday with girls will be a nightmare. And it is, because he's fallen for his stepsister. Can it get any worse? Find out in *You Can't Fancy Your Stepsister*

 3. Lissie's half-sister is a spoilt brat, but her mum thinks she's adorable. Can Lissie make her see what's really going on? Find out in *She's No Angel*

4. Becca's mum describes her boy-friend's daughter as perfect in every way. Can Becca bear to meet her? Find out in *Too Good To Be True*

 5. Ed's stepsisters are getting seriously on his nerves. Should he go and live with his mum? Find out in *Get Me Out Of Here*

 6. Hannah and Rachel are stepsisters. They're also best friends. What will happen to them if their parents split up? Find out in *Parents Behaving Badly*

 7. When Bethany discovers the truth about Robby, she knows her family will go ballistic. Is it possible to keep his secret from them? Find out in *Don't Tell Mum*

8. Ryan's life is made hell by his bullying stepbrother. Has he got the guts to stand up for himself? Find out in *Losing My Identity*

 9. Katie knows it's wrong to lie to her mum. Will she decide to own up, despite the consequences? Find out in *Secrets and Lies*

 10. Ashley can't stand her mum's interfering boyfriend. But it's possible she's got him wrong. Has she? Find out in *Healing the Pain*

 11. Joe used to like Eleanor. Now, he's got to live with her. Can he cope? Find out in *She Wants War?*